THE PELICAN SHAKESPEARE

GENERAL EDITOR ALFRED HARBAGE

KING LEAR

WILLIAM SHAKESPEARE

KING LEAR

EDITED BY ALFRED HARBAGE

PENGUIN BOOKS

Penguin Books Ltd, Harmondsworth,
Middlesex, England
Penguin Books, 625 Madison Avenue,
New York, New York 10022, U.S.A.
Penguin Books Australia Ltd, Ringwood,
Victoria, Australia
Penguin Books Canada Limited, 2801 John Street,
Markham, Ontario, Canada L3R 1B4
Penguin Books (N.Z.) Ltd, 182–190 Wairau Road,
Auckland 10, New Zealand

First published in *The Pelican Shakespeare* 1958
This revised edition first published 1970
Reprinted 1973, 1975, 1976, 1977, 1979, 1980 (twice), 1981

Library of Congress catalog card number: 75-98372

Printed in the United States of America by
Kingsport Press, Inc., Kingsport, Tennessee
Set in Monotype Ehrhardt

CONTENTS

PUBLISHER'S NOTE

Soon after the thirty-eight volumes forming *The Pelican Shakespeare* had been published, they were brought together in *The Complete Pelican Shakespeare*. The editorial revisions and new textual features are explained in detail in the General Editor's Preface to the one-volume edition. They have all been incorporated in the present volume. The following should be mentioned in particular:

The lines are not numbered in arbitrary units. Instead all lines are numbered which contain a word, phrase, or allusion explained in the glossarial notes. In the occasional instances where there is a long stretch of unannotated text, certain lines are numbered in italics to serve the conventional reference purpose.

The intrusive and often inaccurate place-headings inserted by early editors are omitted (as is becoming standard practise), but for the convenience of those who miss them, an indication of locale now appears as first item in the annotation of each scene.

In the interest of both elegance and utility, each speech-prefix is set in a separate line when the speaker's lines are in verse, except when these words form the second half of a pentameter line. Thus the verse form of the speech is kept visually intact, and turned-over lines are avoided. What is printed as verse and what is printed as prose has, in general, the authority of the original texts. Departures from the original texts in this regard have only the authority of editorial tradition and the judgment of the Pelican editors; and, in a few instances, are admittedly arbitrary.

SHAKESPEARE AND
HIS STAGE

William Shakespeare was christened in Holy Trinity
Church, Stratford-upon-Avon, April 26, 1564. His birth
is traditionally assigned to April 23. He was the eldest of
four boys and two girls who survived infancy in the family
of John Shakespeare, glover and trader of Henley Street,
and his wife Mary Arden, daughter of a small landowner
of Wilmcote. In 1568 John was elected Bailiff (equivalent
to Mayor) of Stratford, having already filled the minor
municipal offices. The town maintained for the sons of the
burgesses a free school, taught by a university graduate
and offering preparation in Latin sufficient for university
entrance; its early registers are lost, but there can be little
doubt that Shakespeare received the formal part of his
education in this school.

On November 27, 1582, a license was issued for the
marriage of William Shakespeare (aged eighteen) and Ann
Hathaway (aged twenty-six), and on May 26, 1583, their
child Susanna was christened in Holy Trinity Church.
The inference that the marriage was forced upon the youth
is natural but not inevitable; betrothal was legally binding
at the time, and was sometimes regarded as conferring
conjugal rights. Two additional children of the marriage,
the twins Hamnet and Judith, were christened on Feb-
ruary 2, 1585. Meanwhile the prosperity of the elder
Shakespeares had declined, and William was impelled to
seek a career outside Stratford.

The tradition that he spent some time as a country

teacher is old but unverifiable. Because of the absence of records his early twenties are called the "lost years," and only one thing about them is certain – that at least some of these years were spent in winning a place in the acting profession. He may have begun as a provincial trouper, but by 1592 he was established in London and prominent enough to be attacked. In a pamphlet of that year, *Groats-worth of Wit*, the ailing Robert Greene complained of the neglect which university writers like himself had suffered from actors, one of whom was daring to set up as a playwright:

> . . . an vpstart Crow, beautified with our feathers, that with his *Tygers hart wrapt in a Players hyde*, supposes he is as well able to bombast out a blanke verse as the best of you: and beeing an absolute *Iohannes fac totum*, is in his owne conceit the onely Shake-scene in a countrey.

The pun on his name, and the parody of his line "O tiger's heart wrapped in a woman's hide" (*3 Henry VI*), pointed clearly to Shakespeare. Some of his admirers protested, and Henry Chettle, the editor of Greene's pamphlet, saw fit to apologize:

> . . . I am as sory as if the originall fault had beene my fault, because my selfe haue seene his demeanor no lesse ciuill than he excelent in the qualitie he professes: Besides, diuers of worship haue reported his vprightnes of dealing, which argues his honesty, and his facetious grace in writting, that approoues his Art. (Prefatory epistle, *Kind-Harts Dreame*)

The plague closed the London theatres for many months in 1592–94, denying the actors their livelihood. To this period belong Shakespeare's two narrative poems, *Venus and Adonis* and *The Rape of Lucrece*, both dedicated to the Earl of Southampton. No doubt the poet was rewarded with a gift of money as usual in such cases, but he did no further dedicating and we have no reliable information on whether Southampton, or anyone else, became his regular patron. His sonnets, first mentioned in 1598 and published without his consent in 1609, are intimate without being explicitly autobiographical. They seem to commemorate the poet's friendship with an idealized youth, rivalry with a more favored poet, and love affair with a dark mistress; and his bitterness when the mistress betrays him in conjunction with the friend; but it is difficult to decide precisely what the "story" is, impossible to decide whether it is fictional or true. The true distinction of the sonnets, at least of those not purely conventional, rests in the universality of the thoughts and moods they express, and in their poignancy and beauty.

In 1594 was formed the theatrical company known until 1603 as the Lord Chamberlain's men, thereafter as the King's men. Its original membership included, besides Shakespeare, the beloved clown Will Kempe and the famous actor Richard Burbage. The company acted in various London theatres and even toured the provinces, but it is chiefly associated in our minds with the Globe Theatre built on the south bank of the Thames in 1599. Shakespeare was an actor and joint owner of this company (and its Globe) through the remainder of his creative years. His plays, written at the average rate of two a year, together with Burbage's acting won it its place of leadership among the London companies.

Individual plays began to appear in print, in editions both honest and piratical, and the publishers became increasingly aware of the value of Shakespeare's name on the title pages. As early as 1598 he was hailed as the leading English dramatist in the *Palladis Tamia* of Francis Meres:

As *Plautus* and *Seneca* are accounted the best for Comedy and Tragedy among the Latines, so *Shakespeare* among the English is the most excellent in both kinds for the stage: for Comedy, witnes his *Gentlemen of Verona*, his *Errors*, his *Loue labors lost*, his *Loue labours wonne* [at one time in print but no longer extant, at least under this title], his *Midsummers night dream*, & his *Merchant of Venice*; for Tragedy, his *Richard the 2*, *Richard the 3*, *Henry the 4*, *King Iohn*, *Titus Andronicus*, and his *Romeo and Iuliet*.

The note is valuable both in indicating Shakespeare's prestige and in helping us to establish a chronology. In the second half of his writing career, history plays gave place to the great tragedies; and farces and light comedies gave place to the problem plays and symbolic romances. In 1623, seven years after his death, his former fellow-actors, John Heminge and Henry Condell, cooperated with a group of London printers in bringing out his plays in collected form. The volume is generally known as the First Folio.

Shakespeare had never severed his relations with Stratford. His wife and children may sometimes have shared his London lodgings, but their home was Stratford. His son Hamnet was buried there in 1596, and his daughters Susanna and Judith were married there in 1607 and 1616 respectively. (His father, for whom he had secured a coat of arms and thus the privilege of writing himself gentleman, died in 1601, his mother in 1608.) His considerable earnings in London, as actor-sharer, part owner of the Globe, and playwright, were invested chiefly in Stratford property. In 1597 he purchased for £60 New Place, one of the two most imposing residences in the town. A number of other business transactions, as well as minor episodes in his career, have left documentary records. By 1611 he was in a position to retire, and he seems gradually to have withdrawn from theatrical activity in order to live in Stratford. In March, 1616, he made a will, leaving token bequests to Burbage, Heminge, and Condell, but the bulk of his estate to his family. The most famous feature of the will, the bequest of the second-best bed to his wife, reveals nothing about Shakespeare's marriage; the quaintness of the provision seems commonplace to those familiar with ancient testaments. Shakespeare died April 23, 1616, and was buried in the Stratford church where he had been christened. Within seven years a monument was erected to his memory on the north wall of the chancel. Its portrait bust and the Droeshout engraving on the title page of the First Folio provide the only likenesses with an established claim to authenticity. The best verbal vignette was written by his rival Ben Jonson, the more impressive for being imbedded in a context mainly critical:

> . . . I loved the man, and doe honour his memory (on this side idolatry) as much as any. Hee was indeed honest, and of an open and free nature: had an excellent Phantsie, brave notions, and gentle expressions. . . . (*Timber or Discoveries*, ca. 1623–30)

*

The reader of Shakespeare's plays is aided by a general knowledge of the way in which they were staged. The King's men acquired a roofed and artificially lighted theatre only toward the close of Shakespeare's career, and then only for winter use. Nearly all his plays were designed for performance in such structures as the Globe – a three-tiered amphitheatre with a large rectangular platform extending to the center of its yard. The plays were staged by daylight, by large casts brilliantly costumed, but with only a minimum of properties, without scenery, and quite possibly without intermissions. There was a rear stage gallery for action "above," and a curtained rear recess for "discoveries" and other special effects, but by far the major portion of any play was enacted upon the projecting platform, with episode following episode in swift succession, and with shifts of time and place signaled the audience only by the momentary clearing of the stage between the episodes. Information about the identity of the characters and, when necessary, about the time and place of the action was incorporated in the dialogue. No place-headings have been inserted in the present editions; these are apt to obscure the original fluidity of structure, with the emphasis upon action and speech rather than scenic background. (Indications of place are supplied in the footnotes.) The acting, including that of the youthful apprentices to the profession who performed the parts of women, was highly skillful, with a premium placed upon grace of gesture and beauty of diction. The audiences, a cross section of the general public, commonly numbered a thousand, sometimes more than two thousand. Judged by the type of plays they applauded, these audiences were not only large but also perceptive.

THE TEXTS OF THE PLAYS

About half of Shakespeare's plays appeared in print for the first time in the folio volume of 1623. The others had been published individually, usually in quarto volumes, during his lifetime or in the six years following his death. The copy used by the printers of the quartos varied greatly in merit, sometimes representing Shakespeare's true text, sometimes only a debased version of that text. The copy used by the printers of the folio also varied in merit, but was chosen with care. Since it consisted of the best available manuscripts, or the more acceptable quartos (although frequently in editions other than the first), or of quartos corrected by reference to manuscripts, we have good or reasonably good texts of most of the thirty-seven plays.

In the present series, the plays have been newly edited from quarto or folio texts, depending, when a choice offered, upon which is now regarded by bibliographical specialists as the more authoritative. The ideal has been to reproduce the chosen texts with as few alterations as possible, beyond occasional relineation, expansion of abbreviations, and modernization of punctuation and spelling. Emendation is held to a minimum, and such material as has been added, in the way of stage directions and lines supplied by an alternative text, has been enclosed in square brackets.

None of the plays printed in Shakespeare's lifetime were divided into acts and scenes, and the inference is that the author's own manuscripts were not so divided. In the folio collection, some of the plays remained undivided, some were divided into acts, and some were divided into acts and scenes. During the eighteenth century all of the plays were divided into acts and scenes, and in the Cambridge edition of the mid-nineteenth century, from which the influential Globe text derived, this division was more or less regularized and the lines were numbered. Many useful works of reference employ the act–scene–line apparatus thus established.

Since this act–scene division is obviously convenient, but is of very dubious authority so far as Shakespeare's own structural principles are concerned, or the original manner of staging his plays, a problem is presented to modern editors. In the present series the act–scene division is retained marginally, and may be viewed as a reference aid like the line numbering. A star marks the points of division when these points have been determined by a cleared stage indicating a shift of time and place in the action of the play, or when no harm results from the editorial assumption that there is such a shift. However, at those points where the established division is clearly misleading – that is, where continuous action has been split up into separate "scenes" – the star is omitted and the distortion corrected. This mechanical expedient seemed the best means of combining utility and accuracy.

THE GENERAL EDITOR

INTRODUCTION

The play begins with a moment of prose "exposition," an idle conversation about the partition of a kingdom and the bastardy of a son. Its tone is casual, jocular, polite. The son responds decorously to a social introduction. The speakers are wearing familiar masks. It is then as if these murmurs by the portal subsided at the opening of some old but half-remembered ceremony. All is ritual – heralding trumpet, formal procession, symbolic objects in coronet and map, a sequence of arbitrary yet strangely predictable acts. What can be made of it? Why should that patriarch who wishes to yield up his power and possessions require of the receivers declarations of love? Why should that maiden who honestly loves him respond only with declarations of her love of honesty? No logical reasons appear – ritual is ritual, its logic its own. Prose is yielding to poetry, "realism" to reality. *King Lear* is not true. It is an allegory of truth.

That its truths are not literal is the first thing about it discerned by the budding critical faculty. Everything is initially *patterned* – this one making obvious errors which he obviously will rue, these others emerging as the good and the evil in almost geometrical symmetry, with the inevitable sisters-three, the two elder chosen though wicked, the younger rejected though virtuous. Surely these are childish things! A defense has been offered by Tolstoy, in his valedictory judgment that the only truths conveyable in literature can be conveyed in the simplest folk-tale. But *King Lear* is not simple, and Tolstoy himself failed to see its relevance to his doctrine. Freud noticed its primitive features, and compared Goneril, Regan, and Cordelia to the caskets of lead, silver, and gold in *The Merchant of Venice*. He identified Cordelia as the benign, though resisted, call of death. Cordelia as the death-wish – *lovely and soothing death* – how suggestive this is! until we recognize that her identification as the life-wish might be equally suggestive. The value of such reflections lies in their reminder that the oldest story-patterns have the greatest power to touch off reverberations. No other framework than this parable-myth could have borne so well the weight of what Shakespeare was compelled to say.

The story of Lear and his three daughters was given written form four centuries before Shakespeare's birth. How much older its components may be we do not know. Cordelia in one guise or another, including Cinderella's, has figured in the folklore of most cultures, perhaps originally expressing what Emerson saw as the conviction of every human being of his worthiness to be loved and chosen, if only his *true* self were truly known. The figure of the ruler asking a question, often a riddle, with disastrous consequences to himself is equally old and dispersed. In his *Historia Regum Britanniae* (1136) Geoffrey of Monmouth converted folklore to history and established Lear and his daughters as rulers of ancient Britain, thus bequeathing them to the chronicles. Raphael Holinshed's (1587) declared that "Leir, the sonne of Baldud," came to the throne "in the yeare of the world 3105, at what time Joas reigned in Juda," but belief in the historicity of such British kings was now beginning to wane, and Shakespeare could deal freely with the record. He read the story also in John Higgins' lamentable verses in *The Firste part of the Mirour for Magistrates* (1574), and in Edmund Spenser's *Faerie Queene*, II, 10, 27–32. He knew, and may even have acted in, a bland dramatic version, *The True Chronicle History of King Leir*, published anonymously in 1605 but staged at least as early as 1594.

The printing of the old play may mark an effort to capitalize upon the staging of Shakespeare's, performed at court on December 26, 1606, and probably first brought out at the Globe playhouse sometime in 1605, although its allusion to "these late eclipses of the sun and moon" was not necessarily suggested by those of September and October of that year. The only certain anterior limit of date is March 16, 1603, when Samuel Harsnett's *Declaration of Egregious Popishe Impostures* was registered for publication. That this excursion in "pseudo-demonology" was available to Shakespeare is evident in various ways, most clearly in the borrowed inventory of devils imbedded in Edgar's jargon as Tom o' Bedlam. It is of small consequence to fix the date of *King Lear* so far as its relation to the older play is concerned, which must be reckoned as analogue rather than source, but if, as seems certain, it was composed in 1605 or early 1606, it belongs to the same season of the poet's growth as *The Tragedy of Macbeth*.

In its pre-Shakespearean forms, both those mentioned above and others, the Lear story remains rudimentary. The emphasis may vary in various recensions, depending upon whether the author was most interested in the inexpedience of subdividing a kingdom, the mutability of fortune, or, as in the older play, the rewards of Christian virtue; but all are alike in that they end happily for Lear, who is reconciled to Cordelia and restored to his throne. The fact that the story was sometimes followed by a sequel in which Cordelia was finally hounded to suicide by the broodlings of her wicked sisters has little bearing on a remarkable fact: Shakespeare alone and in defiance of precedent conducted Lear to ultimate misery. *Enter Lear, with Cordelia in his arms. . . . He dies.* These directions enclose a scene which demonstrates beyond any other in tragic literature the intransigence of poetic art – inventing the inevitable, investing horrifying things with beauty.

Compared with the tragedies of ancient Greece – and it is with these alone that one is tempted to compare it – *King Lear* suggests the Gothic order. Its form is irregular and organic, determined seemingly by a series of upward thrusts of mounting internal energy. There is even a Gothic element of the grotesque, as when mock-beggar, jester, and king, reduced to common condition, hold their mad juridical proceedings in a storm-lashed shelter, or when crazed king and blinded subject exchange lamentations and puns! In the method of Lear's madness there is often a savage humor, more remarkable when all is said than his companioning with a Fool. It was the Fool, however, who seemed to the next age the unpardonable sin against classical decorum. In the 1680 adaptation by Nahum Tate he was expunged from the play, along with the tragic ending. Tate capped the concluding felicities of the pre-Shakespearean versions by huddling up a marriage between Edgar and Cordelia; yet his work held the stage throughout the eighteenth century. It is always ruefully remarked that the greatest critic of the age approved the adaptation, but in fairness we should add that it was not for literary reasons. The pain of Shakespeare's concluding scenes was simply too much for Dr Johnson; his response is preferable to that of those – fit for treasons, stratagems, and spoils – who can read these scenes unmoved.

The original play, or its approximation, was restored to the stage in the early nineteenth century, after it had begun to receive its critical due from the romantic essayists and poets. It is a poet's play. Keats saw in it the warrant for his conviction that truth and beauty are one, and, more surprisingly, recognized the choral and catalytic function of Lear's jester for the stroke of genius it is. Coleridge, Lamb, and Hazlitt also recorded illuminating judgments, and many critics since, of many different "schools," have said fine things about it.

The question now most frequently debated is whether the play is Christian and affirmative in spirit, or pagan and pessimistic. No work of art could endure the tugs of such a debate without being somewhat torn. "Pessimistic," like "optimistic," is a small word for a small thing, and *King Lear* is not small. It is sad, as all tragedies are sad. It is religious, as all great tragedies are religious. The exclusion of specific Christian reference, more consistent than in any other Shakespearean play of non-Christian setting, is in harmony with its Old Testament atmosphere (when "Joas reigned in Juda"), but it may reflect nothing more than evasion, in the printed text, of a recent Parliamentary ruling, which in effect labelled *God* in stage speech as blasphemy, *gods* as mere classical allusion. Although the play is rather inclusively than exclusively Christian, which can scarcely be deemed a fault, it shows obvious signs of its genesis in a Christian culture. To cite those involving a single character (other than Cordelia, who has often been viewed as a Christ-symbol), there is Edgar's persistence in returning good for evil, his preachments against the sin of despair, and his reluctance to kill except in trial by combat with its implied religious sanctions. Great questions are asked of the unseen powers – "Is there any cause in nature that makes these hard hearts?" – and these questions remain unanswered, but the silence which follows them should be viewed, here as in other contexts, as the substance of faith. On the human level, the implications of the play are more comforting than the data it abstracts. In our actual world, suffering is not always ennobling, evil not always self-consuming. In every scene where there is pain, there is someone who strives to relieve that pain. At the close, the merciless have all perished; the last sound we hear is the choral voices of the merciful.

The workers of evil are stylized in a way not quite typical of Shakespeare. He could not love these characters even as characters, except perhaps Edmund a little. To imitate the dominant animal imagery of the style, Cornwall is less repellent than Goneril and Regan only as the mad bull is less repellent than the hyena, they less repellent than Oswald only as the hyena is less repellent than the jackal. To the latter he failed to give even that engaging touch of the ludicrous he usually reserved for assistant villains. It is useless to speak of their "motivation." Like other aged parents Lear is no gift to good housewifery, and there is something poignantly familiar about such a one's trudging resentfully to the home of a second daughter. "Age is unnecessary." But to see a causal relationship between what he does to Goneril and Regan and what they do to him, or to interpret their aggression as normal revolt against parental domination, is simply to be perverse. The play deals directly, and in both its stories, with one indissoluble bond:

> We'll no more meet, no more see one another.
> But yet thou art my flesh, my blood, my daughter....

Eroded, it leaves no human bond secure. To argue that Edmund's conduct is attributable to humiliating illegitimacy, we must supply him with an "unconscious" and invoke its spectral evidence; there is no sign of sensitivity in his lines. Even that curious product of our times, the liberalism-gone-to-seed which automatically defends anything from treachery to sadism providing it savors of non-conformity, has found little to say for this insatiable quintet.

Shakespeare is not normally associated with hatred, but "a fierce hatred of cruelty and deceitful wickedness" informs *King Lear* – this the opinion of so pure an aesthetician as Benedetto Croce. Hazlitt has said, "It is then the best of all Shakespeare's plays, for it is the one in which he was most in earnest." A non-sequitur may lurk in this assertion, but we cannot deny its relevance. Our inescapable impression of the play is of its overwhelming sincerity. It says everything powerfully and everything twice – and always "what we feel, not what we ought to say." The language varies from the cryptic allusiveness of Lear's "mad" speeches to the biblical plainness of his pleas for forgiveness; and though it is often difficult, it is never ambiguous. Lamb has been much taken to task for declaring that "*Lear* is essentially impossible to be represented on a stage," but more often than not our experiences in the theatre confirm his view. There have been fine productions, but not very many : one touch of insincerity can rot everything away.

Those who now "introduce" this play must wish with Hazlitt, and with much more likelihood of greeting the wish of the reader, that they might resort to silence, since all that can be said will "fall short of the subject, or even what we ourselves conceive of it." Yet an effort must be made to state its theme, and to the present editor there seems no way of doing this except by focussing the gaze directly and continuously upon Lear himself.

"The King is coming." These words announce the first entrance of the tragic hero. Let us see him as he is, no preconceptions or critical rumors spoiling the innocence of our vision. Nothing about him suggests infirmity or decay. His magnitude and force are far greater than one's own. He issues commands with the assurance of instinct and lifelong custom. He holds a map in his hands like a Titan holding a kingdom. The kingdom spreads before us in his spacious utterance :

> Of all these bounds, even from this line to this,
> With shadowy forests and with champains riched,
> With plenteous rivers and wide-skirted meads,
> We make thee lady.

We make thee lady! Thus he disposes of a sector of the earth, this ring-giver, this warrior-leader, this chosen one, his only landlord God! Is it not passing fine . . .? Here is no soft-brained *Senex*, but the archetypal *King*.

As such Lear symbolizes Mankind, and we will say nothing essential about him by reckoning up his years and growing glib about the symptoms of senile dementia. The king-figure surrogate is an understandable product of the human mind in its early attempts at abstraction, since the most imposing of single men best lends his image to the difficult concept of Man. His vicissitudes best epitomize the vicissitudes of all, since upon the highest altitude the sun shines brightest and the cold snow lies most deep. Early Renaissance drama was steeped in the tradition of this symbolic figure, sometimes still called *King* as well as *Mankind*, *Everyman*, *Genus Humanum*, and the like. He is always identifiable by his centrality in the action, and the mixed company he keeps – vices or flatterers on the one hand, virtues or truth-speakers on the other. And there stands Lear – Goneril and Regan to the left, Kent and Cordelia to the right.

But this is also a family gathering. There is the father, and there the servants and children of his house. The central figure is, and seems always more so as the play weaves its spell, not only archetypal King, Man, and Father, but particular king, man, and father. No symbol that remained purely symbol could so touch our emotions. To have children of his flesh and blood, the father must be flesh and blood – such as can be old, grow weary, feel cold and wet.

Only a few days of fictional time elapse, only a few hours in the theatre, so that Lear's first words still echo in our ears as we hear his last.

We make thee lady.... Let it be so, thy truth then be thy dower! ... Peace, Kent! Come not between the dragon and his wrath.... The bow is bent and drawn; make from the shaft.... Therefore be gone.... Let me not stay a jot for dinner; go get it ready.... Call the clotpoll back.

Such are Lear's accents at the beginning. And at the close –

You must bear with me.... I am old and foolish.... Her voice was ever soft, gentle, and low. . . . Pray you undo this button. Thank you, sir.

He has learned a new language. We are required to accept this learning as good, but we are forbidden to rejoice.

The play is Lear's gethsemane, its great reality his suffering, which so draws us into itself that our conception of the work as a whole is formed in the crucible of our fear and pity. His anguish is kin with the anguish of Job, Prometheus, Oedipus, and other tragic projections of spirits in agony, but it retains its own peculiar quality. Its cause, its nature, and its meaning will always remain the imperfectly resolved crux of the play; and one can do no more than explain, with such confidence as one is able to muster, how these things appear to him.

To say that Lear gets what he deserves is to share the opinion of Goneril and Regan. (Some have even implied that Cordelia gets what she deserves, anaesthetizing their heads and hearts with obtuse moralisms suggested by the doctrine of "poetic justice.") What does Lear deserve? He is proud and peremptory, and it is better to be humble and temporizing, but there are occupational hazards in being a king, perhaps even in being a father. Is his charge not true that the world has lied to him, telling him he was wise before he was bearded, returning "yea and nay" to everything he said? His guilt is widely shared, and his "flaw" like that of Oedipus seems mysteriously hereditary. And it is linked inextricably with his virtues. We applaud the resurgence of youthful might that cuts down Cordelia's assassin. We admire the valor of his attempts (and they come quite early) to be patient, to compromise, to hold back womanish tears, to cling to his reason. Nothing is more moving than his bewildered attempts to meet "social" obligations as he kneels by Cordelia's body. We love his *manliness*. Pride has its value too.

Lear's errors stem from no corruption of heart. His rejection of Kent and Cordelia is the reflex of his attachment to them. The errors are not the man. The man is one who has valued and been valued by such as they. The things he wants – fidelity and love – are good things. That he should find them in his servant and his child seems to him an aspect of universal order. In his vocabulary, as distinct from Edmund's, such things are *natural*. His inability to distinguish between the false and the true, and his craving for visible displays, are not failings peculiar to him. "How much do you love me?" – few parents suppress this bullying question, spoken or unspoken, however much they may have felt its burden as children. It seems in the nature of some things that they always be learned too late, that as children we might have offered more, as parents demanded less. To punish a thankless child has the appearance of justice, to withdraw in one's age from the cares of state the appearance of wisdom, to dispose of one's goods by gift instead of testament the appearance of generosity. Plain men in their prime have been similarly deceived. Gloucester shakes his head sadly over Lear's injustice, folly, and selfishness as he duplicates his actions.

In the maimed but agile mind of the Fool faithfully dogging Lear's steps, his errors stand as an *idée fixe* and are harped upon with terrible iteration. We should not imitate the example. We may find more meaning in the excess of expiation. The purely physical suffering – denial of rest, exposure to wind and rain – is real, but it strikes the sufferer himself as little more than a metaphor. We may say that his spiritual suffering is in excess of his actual afflictions, that it is selfish and centrifugal, or a mere symptom of aged petulance, but if we do so, we are stopping our ears to the voice of Shakespeare and all his decent spokesmen. Lear's curse of Goneril is still alienating, like his treatment of Cordelia, but when he stands weeping before his cormorant daughters in whom he has put his faith, and they coolly and relentlessly strip him of every vestige of dignity, our hearts turn over. Humility may be good, but this humiliation is evil.

There is no *need* that this man be attended by a hundred knights, that his messenger be deferentially treated, or that his children offer him more than subsistence. His cause rests upon no more rational grounds than our powers of sympathy and imagination. "O reason not the need." As his every expectation is brutally defeated, and he looks in dazed recognition upon the world as it is instead of what he thought it was, of himself as he is instead of what he thought he was, we defer to his past illusions. He had never identified prestige merely as power, had never imagined that the visages of respect, kindliness, and love could contort into the hideous lines of icy contempt and sour indifference.

Lear's anguish now represents for us Man's horror and sense of helplessness at the discovery of evil – the infiltration of animality in the human world, naked cruelty and appetite. It is a fissure that threatens to widen infinitely, and we see Lear at the center of turbulence as it works its breakage in minds, in families, in nations, in the heavens themselves, interacting in dreadful concatenation.

The significance of Lear's response to his discovery is best seen in the light of Gloucester's. In Sidney's *Arcadia*, II, 10, the "storie of the Paphlagonian unkind King and his kinde sonne" repeats in essence the Lear legend, except that the children, false and true, are sons instead of daughters. By reducing the rank of Sidney's king and interweaving his parallel fate in alternate scenes, Shakespeare is able, amazingly, both further to universalize and further to particularize the experience of Lear. Gloucester also represents Man, but his distinction from Lear suggests the distinction between ordinary and extraordinary men. Gloucester is amiably confused about the tawdriness of his past, of which Edmund is the product, and sentimentally fumbling in the present. What appears in Lear as heroic error appears in him as gullibility. His fine moments are identical with those of a nameless serf of Cornwall's and an ancient tenant of his own – in the presence of cruelty he becomes kind and brave :

GLOUCESTER I am tied to th' stake, and I must stand the course.
REGAN Wherefore to Dover ?
GLOUCESTER Because I would not see thy cruel nails
   Pluck out his poor old eyes.

Like Lear he is incorrupt of heart, and he grows in dignity, but his total response to vicious encroachment is something akin to apathy and surrender; his instinct is to retreat.

Not so with Lear. He batters himself to pieces against the fact of evil. Granted that its disruptive power has been unleashed by his own error, so that error itself partakes of evil, as he is shudderingly aware, yet he remains the great antagonist. Falsity, cruelty, injustice, corruption – their appalling forms swir¹ about him in phantasmic patterns. His instinct is to rip them from the universe, to annihilate all things if it is the only way to annihilate these things. His charges of universal hypocrisy : "handy-dandy, which is the justice, which is the thief?" – his denial of human responsibility : "None does offend, none – I say none!" – his indictment of life itself :

   Thou know'st, the first time that we smell the air
   We wawl and cry –

cancel their own nihilism, because they sound no acquiescence. Lear is the voice of protest. The grandeur of his spirit supplies the impotence of his body as he opposes to evil all that is left him to oppose – his molten indignation, his huge invectives, his capacity for feeling pain.

This quality of Lear seen in retrospect, his hunger after righteousness, gives magnitude to the concluding scenes. His spirit has been doubly lacerated by his own sense of guilt. He has failed "poor naked wretches" no different from himself, and he has wronged Cordelia. His remorse has found expression only in brief occasional utterances, welling up as it were against desperate efforts of containment, but its scalding power is revealed in his acts of abasement when he and Cordelia meet. The final episodes are all vitally linked. When the two are led in captive, we are made to look back upon their reunion, which he dreams of endlessly reenacting:

> When thou dost ask me blessing, I'll kneel down
> And ask of thee forgiveness;

then forward to their death:

> Upon such sacrifices, my Cordelia,
> The gods themselves throw incense.

The words help to effect that perfect coalescence of particular and general tragic experience achieved as he kneels beside her body. This is a father and his child who will come no more, the father remembering his own unkindness and the child's endearing ways. There is no melioration in his dying delusion that she still lives, no mention of an after-life. It is unspeakably sad. But it merges with a larger yet less devastating sadness. This is also a sacrifice, and although the somber tones of the survivors as they take up the burden of survival give it relevance to the future as well as the past, it is such a sacrifice as obliquely vindicates the gods if upon it they throw incense.

We know, not as an item of faith but of simple demonstrable fact, that we are greatly indebted for such wisdom as we have, that it was bought with "sacrifices." In the struggle of our kind against brutality, the great casualties, spiritual and even physical, have always been among those who have been best and those who have cared most. In the world of this play Cordelia has brought us the truest sense of human goodness, her words "No cause, no cause" the truest sense of moral beauty. She is the perfect offering. And so is Lear. She is best. He cares most for what is best. The play ends as it begins in an allegorical grouping, commemorating humanity's long, agonized, and continuing struggle to be human. This larger meaning gives our tears the dignity of an act of ratification and gratitude: to these still figures we have pitied we owe the gift of feeling pity.

Harvard University   ALFRED HARBAGE

NOTE ON THE TEXT

In 1608 a version of *King Lear* appeared in a quarto volume sold by Nathaniel Butter at his shop at the Pied Bull. Its text was reproduced in 1619 in a quarto falsely dated 1608. Various theories have been offered to explain the nature of the Pied Bull text, the most recent being that it represents Shakespeare's rough draft carelessly copied, and corrupted by the faulty memories of actors who were party to the copying. In 1623 a greatly improved though "cut" version of the play appeared in the first folio, evidently printed from the quarto after it had been carefully collated with the official playhouse manuscript. The present edition follows the folio text, and although it adds in square brackets the passages appearing only in the quarto, and accepts fifty-three quarto readings, it follows the chosen text more closely than do most recent editions. However, deference to the quarto is paid in an appendix, where its alternative readings, both those accepted and those rejected, are listed. Few editorial emendations have been retained, but see I, ii, 21 *top* (Q & F 'to'), II, ii, 138 *contemnèd'st* (Q 'temnest'), III, vi, 25 *bourn* (Q 'broom'), III, vi, 67 *lym* (Q & F 'him'), IV, ii, 57 *to threat* (Q 'thereat'), IV, iii, 20 *seemed* (Q 'seeme'), 31 *moistened* (Q 'moistened her'). The quarto text is not divided into acts and scenes. The act and scene division here supplied marginally for reference purposes is that of the folio except that Act II, Scene ii of the latter has been subdivided into Scenes ii, iii, and iv. The continuity of the action here, and at several other misleadingly divided sections of the play, is indicated in the manner explained at the end of "The texts of the plays."

KING LEAR

Lear, King of Britain
King of France
Duke of Burgundy
Duke of Cornwall
Duke of Albany
Earl of Kent
Earl of Gloucester
Edgar, son to Gloucester
Edmund, bastard son to Gloucester
Curan, a courtier
Old Man, tenant to Gloucester
Doctor
Lear's Fool
Oswald, steward to Goneril
A Captain under Edmund's command
Gentlemen loyal to Lear
A Gentleman attending on Cordelia
A Herald
Servants to Cornwall
Goneril
Regan } *daughters to Lear*
Cordelia
Knights attending on Lear, Officers,
 Messengers, Soldiers, Attendants

Scene : *Britain*]

KING LEAR

Enter Kent, Gloucester, and Edmund.

KENT I thought the King had more affected the Duke of
Albany than Cornwall.

GLOUCESTER It did always seem so to us; but now, in the
division of the kingdom, it appears not which of the
dukes he values most, for equalities are so weighed that
curiosity in neither can make choice of either's moiety.

KENT Is not this your son, my lord?

GLOUCESTER His breeding, sir, hath been at my charge.
I have so often blushed to acknowledge him that now I
am brazed to't.

KENT I cannot conceive you.

GLOUCESTER Sir, this young fellow's mother could;
whereupon she grew round-wombed, and had indeed,
sir, a son for her cradle ere she had a husband for her
her bed. Do you smell a fault?

KENT I cannot wish the fault undone, the issue of it being
so proper.

GLOUCESTER But I have a son, sir, by order of law, some
year elder than this who yet is no dearer in my account:
though this knave came something saucily to the world

I, i Room of state within King Lear's palace 1 *affected* warmly regarded
2 *Albany* i.e. Scotland (once ruled by 'Albanacte') 5 *equalities . . .
weighed* i.e. the portions weigh so equally 6 *curiosity . . . moiety* careful
analysis by neither can make him prefer the other's portion 8 *breeding*
rearing 10 *brazed* brazened 11 *conceive* understand (with pun following)
17 *proper* handsome 19 *account* estimation 20 *saucily* (1) impertinently,
(2) bawdily

before he was sent for, yet was his mother fair, there was
22   good sport at his making, and the whoreson must be
acknowledged. Do you know this noble gentleman,
Edmund?

EDMUND No, my lord.

GLOUCESTER My Lord of Kent. Remember him here-
after as my honorable friend.

EDMUND My services to your lordship.

KENT I must love you, and sue to know you better.

EDMUND Sir, I shall study deserving.

31   GLOUCESTER He hath been out nine years, and away he
32   shall again.
                  [Sound a] sennet.
        The King is coming.
                  Enter [one bearing a coronet, then] King Lear, [then
                  the Dukes of] Cornwall, [and] Albany, [next]
                  Goneril, Regan, Cordelia, and Attendants.

LEAR
        Attend the lords of France and Burgundy, Gloucester.

GLOUCESTER
        I shall, my lord.   Exit [with Edmund].

LEAR
36   Meantime we shall express our darker purpose.
        Give me the map there. Know that we have divided
38   In three our kingdom; and 'tis our fast intent
        To shake all cares and business from our age,
        Conferring them on younger strengths while we
        Unburdened crawl toward death. Our son of Cornwall,
        And you our no less loving son of Albany,
43   We have this hour a constant will to publish
44   Our daughters' several dowers, that future strife

---

22 *whoreson* (affectionate abuse, but literally applicable, like *knave* above)
31 *out* away (for training, or in military service)   32 *s.d. sennet* trumpet
flourish (heralding a procession)   36 *darker purpose* more secret intention
(to require declarations of affection)   38 *fast* firm   43 *constant . . . publish*
fixed intention to announce   44 *several* individual

May be prevented now. The princes, France and
   Burgundy,
Great rivals in our youngest daughter's love;
Long in our court have made their amorous sojourn,   47
And here are to be answered. Tell me, my daughters
(Since now we will divest us both of rule,
Interest of territory, cares of state),   50
Which of you shall we say doth love us most,
That we our largest bounty may extend
Where nature doth with merit challenge. Goneril,   53
Our eldest-born, speak first.

GONERIL
Sir, I love you more than word can wield the matter;   55
Dearer than eyesight, space, and liberty;   56
Beyond what can be valuèd, rich or rare;
No less than life, with grace, health, beauty, honor;
As much as child e'er loved, or father found;
A love that makes breath poor, and speech unable.   60
Beyond all manner of so much I love you.

CORDELIA [aside]
What shall Cordelia speak? Love, and be silent.

LEAR
Of all these bounds, even from this line to this,
With shadowy forests and with champains riched,   64
With plenteous rivers and wide-skirted meads,   65
We make thee lady. To thine and Albany's issues   66
Be this perpetual. – What says our second daughter,   67
Our dearest Regan, wife of Cornwall?

REGAN
I am made of that self mettle as my sister,
And prize me at her worth. In my true heart   70

---

47 *amorous sojourn* i.e. visit of courtship 50 *Interest* legal possession 53 *nature . . . challenge* natural affection matches other merits 55 *wield* handle 56 *space* scope (for the exercise of *liberty*) 60 *breath* voice; *unable* inadequate 64 *champains riched* plains enriched 65 *wide-skirted* far spreading 66 *issues* descendants 67 *perpetual* in perpetuity 70 *prize . . . worth* value me at her value

71   I find she names my very deed of love;
     Only she comes too short, that I profess
     Myself an enemy to all other joys
74   Which the most precious square of sense possesses,
75   And find I am alone felicitate
     In your dear Highness' love.

CORDELIA [aside]   Then poor Cordelia;
     And yet not so, since I am sure my love's
78   More ponderous than my tongue.

LEAR
     To thee and thine hereditary ever
     Remain this ample third of our fair kingdom,
81   No less in space, validity, and pleasure
     Than that conferred on Goneril. – Now, our joy,
83   Although our last and least; to whose young love
84   The vines of France and milk of Burgundy
85   Strive to be interest; what can you say to draw
     A third more opulent than your sisters? Speak.

CORDELIA
     Nothing, my lord.

LEAR Nothing?

CORDELIA Nothing.

LEAR
     Nothing will come of nothing. Speak again.

CORDELIA
     Unhappy that I am, I cannot heave
     My heart into my mouth. I love your Majesty
93   According to my bond, no more nor less.

LEAR
     How, how, Cordelia? Mend your speech a little,
     Lest you may mar your fortunes.

---

71 *my very deed of* the true fact of my   74 *Which . . . possesses* which the most precise measurement by the senses holds to be most precious   75 *felicitate* made happy   78 *ponderous* weighty   81 *validity* value; *pleasure* pleasing qualities   83 *least* smallest, youngest   84 *vines* vineyards; *milk* pasture-lands (?)   85 *interest* concerned as interested parties   93 *bond* obligation

CORDELIA   Good my lord,
You have begot me, bred me, loved me. I
Return those duties back as are right fit,   97
Obey you, love you, and most honor you.
Why have my sisters husbands if they say
They love you all? Haply, when I shall wed,
That lord whose hand must take my plight shall carry   101
Half my love with him, half my care and duty.
Sure I shall never marry like my sisters,
[To love my father all.]

LEAR
But goes thy heart with this?

CORDELIA   Ay, my good lord.

LEAR
So young, and so untender?

CORDELIA
So young, my lord, and true.

LEAR
Let it be so, thy truth then be thy dower!
For, by the sacred radiance of the sun,
The mysteries of Hecate and the night,   110
By all the operation of the orbs   111
From whom we do exist and cease to be,
Here I disclaim all my paternal care,
Propinquity and property of blood,   114
And as a stranger to my heart and me
Hold thee from this for ever. The barbarous Scythian,   116
Or he that makes his generation messes   117
To gorge his appetite, shall to my bosom
Be as well neighbored, pitied, and relieved,
As thou my sometime daughter.   120

KENT   Good my liege –

---

97 *Return . . . fit* i.e. am fittingly dutiful in return   **101** *plight* pledge, troth-plight   **110** *Hecate* infernal goddess, patroness of witches   **111** *operation . . . orbs* astrological influences   **114** *Propinquity* relationship; *property* i.e. common property, something shared   **116** *Scythian* (proverbially barbarous)   **117** *makes . . . messes* makes meals of his offspring   **120** *sometime* former

LEAR

    Peace, Kent!

122   Come not between the dragon and his wrath.

123   I loved her most, and thought to set my rest

124   On her kind nursery. – Hence and avoid my sight! –

125   So be my grave my peace as here I give

    Her father's heart from her! Call France. Who stirs!

    Call Burgundy. Cornwall and Albany,

    With my two daughters' dowers digest the third;

    Let pride, which she calls plainness, marry her.

    I do invest you jointly with my power,

131   Preeminence, and all the large effects

132   That troop with majesty. Ourself, by monthly course,

    With reservation of an hundred knights,

    By you to be sustained, shall our abode

    Make with you by due turn. Only we shall retain

136   The name, and all th' addition to a king. The sway,

    Revenue, execution of the rest,

    Belovèd sons, be yours; which to confirm,

139   This coronet part between you.

KENT   Royal Lear,

    Whom I have ever honored as my king,

    Loved as my father, as my master followed,

    As my great patron thought on in my prayers –

LEAR

143   The bow is bent and drawn; make from the shaft.

KENT

144   Let it fall rather, though the fork invade

    The region of my heart. Be Kent unmannerly

    When Lear is mad. What wouldst thou do, old man?

    Think'st thou that duty shall have dread to speak

---

122 *his* its   123 *set my rest* (1) risk my stake (a term in the card game primero), (2) rely for my repose   124 *nursery* nursing, care   125 *So . . . peace as* let me rest peacefully in my grave only as   131 *effects* tokens   132 *Ourself* I (royal plural)   136 *th' addition* honors and prerogatives   139 *coronet* (symbol of rule; not necessarily the royal crown)   143 *make* make away   144 *fall* strike; *fork* two-pronged head

When power to flattery bows? To plainness honor 's
   bound
When majesty falls to folly. Reserve thy state,   149
And in thy best consideration check   150
This hideous rashness. Answer my life my judgment,   151
Thy youngest daughter does not love thee least,
Nor are those empty-hearted whose low sounds
Reverb no hollowness.   154

LEAR   Kent, on thy life, no more!

KENT
My life I never held but as a pawn   155
To wage against thine enemies; ne'er fear to lose it,   156
Thy safety being motive.   157

LEAR   Out of my sight!

KENT
See better, Lear, and let me still remain   158
The true blank of thine eye.   159

LEAR
Now by Apollo—

KENT   Now by Apollo, King,
Thou swear'st thy gods in vain.

LEAR   O vassal! Miscreant!   161
   [Grasping his sword.]

ALBANY, CORNWALL Dear sir, forbear!

KENT
Kill thy physician, and thy fee bestow
Upon the foul disease. Revoke thy gift,
Or, whilst I can vent clamor from my throat,
I'll tell thee thou dost evil.

LEAR   Hear me, recreant,   166
On thine allegiance, hear me!

---

149 *Reserve thy state* retain your kingly authority **150** *best consideration*
most careful deliberation **151** *Answer my life* i.e. I'll stake my life on
154 *Reverb no hollowness* i.e. do not reverberate (like a drum) as a result
of hollowness **155** *pawn* stake **156** *wage* wager, pit **157** *motive* the
moving cause **158** *still* always **159** *blank* center of the target (to guide
your aim truly) **161** *Miscreant* (1) rascal, (2) infidel **166** *recreant* traitor

168 That thou hast sought to make us break our vows,
169 Which we durst never yet, and with strained pride
170 To come betwixt our sentence and our power,
     Which nor our nature nor our place can bear,
172 Our potency made good, take thy reward.
     Five days we do allot thee for provision
174 To shield thee from disasters of the world,
     And on the sixth to turn thy hated back
     Upon our kingdom. If, on the tenth day following,
177 Thy banished trunk be found in our dominions,
     The moment is thy death. Away. By Jupiter,
     This shall not be revoked.

KENT

180 Fare thee well, King. Sith thus thou wilt appear,
     Freedom lives hence, and banishment is here.
          [To Cordelia]
     The gods to their dear shelter take thee, maid,
     That justly think'st and hast most rightly said.
          [To Regan and Goneril]
184 And your large speeches may your deeds approve,
185 That good effects may spring from words of love.
     Thus Kent, O princes, bids you all adieu;
187 He'll shape his old course in a country new.   *Exit.*
          Flourish. Enter Gloucester, with France and
          Burgundy; Attendants.

GLOUCESTER
     Here's France and Burgundy, my noble lord.

LEAR
     My Lord of Burgundy,
     We first address toward you, who with this king
     Hath rivalled for our daughter. What in the least

---

168 *That* in that, since 169 *strained* excessive 170 *To come . . . power*
i.e. to oppose my power to sentence 172 *Our . . . good* if my power is to
be demonstrated as real 174 *disasters* accidents 177 *trunk* body 180
Sith since 184 *approve* confirm 185 *effects* consequences 187 *shape*
. . . course keep to his customary ways (of honesty)

Will you require in present dower with her,
Or cease your quest of love?

BURGUNDY   Most royal Majesty,
I crave no more than hath your Highness offered,
Nor will you tender less.

LEAR   Right noble Burgundy,
When she was dear to us, we did hold her so;
But now her price is fallen. Sir, there she stands.
If aught within that little seeming substance,   198
Or all of it, with our displeasure pieced   199
And nothing more, may fitly like your Grace,
She's there, and she is yours.

BURGUNDY   I know no answer.

LEAR
Will you, with those infirmities she owes,   202
Unfriended, new adopted to our hate,
Dow'red with our curse, and strangered with our oath,   204
Take her, or leave her?

BURGUNDY   Pardon me, royal sir.
Election makes not up on such conditions.   206

LEAR
Then leave her, sir, for by the pow'r that made me
I tell you all her wealth. *[to France]* For you, great King,
I would not from your love make such a stray   209
To match you where I hate; therefore beseech you
T' avert your liking a more worthier way   211
Than on a wretch whom Nature is ashamed
Almost t' acknowledge hers.

FRANCE   This is most strange,
That she whom even but now was your best object,   214
The argument of your praise, balm of your age,   215
The best, the dearest, should in this trice of time

---

198 *seeming substance* i.e. nothing, mere shell   **199** *pieced* joined   **202** *owes* owns   **204** *strangered with* made alien by   **206** *Election . . . conditions* no choice is possible on such terms   **209** *make . . . stray* stray so far as   **211** *avert* turn   **214** *best* favorite   **215** *argument* theme

217   Commit a thing so monstrous to dismantle
       So many folds of favor. Sure her offense
       Must be of such unnatural degree
220   That monsters it, or your fore-vouched affection
221   Fall'n into taint ; which to believe of her
222   Must be a faith that reason without miracle
       Should never plant in me.

CORDELIA   I yet beseech your Majesty,
       If for I want that glib and oily art
225   To speak and purpose not since what I well intend
       I'll do't before I speak, that you make known
       It is no vicious blot, murder or foulness,
       No unchaste action or dishonorèd step,
       That hath deprived me of your grace and favor ;
       But even for want of that for which I am richer –
231   A still-soliciting eye, and such a tongue
       That I am glad I have not, though not to have it
       Hath lost me in your liking.

LEAR   Better thou
       Hadst not been born than not t' have pleased me better.

FRANCE
235   Is it but this ? A tardiness in nature
236   Which often leaves the history unspoke
       That it intends to do. My Lord of Burgundy,
       What say you to the lady ? Love 's not love
239   When it is mingled with regards that stands
       Aloof from th' entire point. Will you have her ?
       She is herself a dowry.

---

217 *to dismantle* so to strip off   **220** *That monsters it* as makes it monstrous (i.e. abnormal, freakish); *fore-vouched* previously sworn   **221** *taint* decay (with the implication that the affection, and the oath attesting it, were tainted in the first place)   **222** *reason . . . miracle* i.e. rational, unaided by miraculous, means of persuasion   **225** *purpose not* i.e. without intending to act in accordance with my words   **231** *still-soliciting* always-begging   **235** *tardiness in nature* natural reticence   **236** *history unspoke* actions unannounced   **239–40** *mingled . . . point* i.e. mixed with irrelevant considerations

BURGUNDY   Royal King,
  Give but that portion which yourself proposed,
  And here I take Cordelia by the hand,
  Duchess of Burgundy.

LEAR
  Nothing. I have sworn. I am firm.

BURGUNDY
  I am sorry then you have so lost a father
  That you must lose a husband.

CORDELIA   Peace be with Burgundy.
  Since that respects of fortune are his love,   248
  I shall not be his wife.

FRANCE
  Fairest Cordelia, that art most rich being poor,
  Most choice forsaken, and most loved despised,
  Thee and thy virtues here I seize upon.
  Be it lawful I take up what's cast away.
  Gods, gods ! 'Tis strange that from their cold'st neglect
  My love should kindle to inflamed respect.   255
  Thy dow'rless daughter, King, thrown to my chance,
  Is queen of us, of ours, and our fair France.
  Not all the dukes of wat'rish Burgundy   258
  Can buy this unprized precious maid of me.   259
  Bid them farewell, Cordelia, though unkind.
  Thou losest here, a better where to find.   261

LEAR
  Thou hast her, France ; let her be thine, for we
  Have no such daughter, nor shall ever see
  That face of hers again. Therefore be gone
  Without our grace, our love, our benison.   265
  Come, noble Burgundy.
                 Flourish. Exeunt [Lear, Burgundy, Cornwall,
                        Albany, Gloucester, and Attendants].

248 *respects* considerations 255 *inflamed respect* ardent regard 258
wat'rish (1) watery, weak, (2) watered, diluted 259 *unprized* unvalued
261 *here* this place; *where* other place 265 *benison* blessing

FRANCE
Bid farewell to your sisters.

CORDELIA
268   The jewels of our father, with washed eyes
       Cordelia leaves you. I know you what you are;
270   And, like a sister, am most loath to call
271   Your faults as they are named. Love well our father.
272   To your professèd bosoms I commit him;
       But yet, alas, stood I within his grace,
274   I would prefer him to a better place.
       So farewell to you both.

REGAN
Prescribe not us our duty.

GONERIL   Let your study
Be to content your lord, who hath received you
278   At fortune's alms. You have obedience scanted,
279   And well are worth the want that you have wanted.

CORDELIA
280   Time shall unfold what plighted cunning hides,
281   Who covers faults, at last with shame derides.
       Well may you prosper.

FRANCE   Come, my fair Cordelia.
                              Exit France and Cordelia.

GONERIL Sister, it is not little I have to say of what most
nearly appertains to us both. I think our father will
hence to-night.

REGAN That's most certain, and with you; next month
with us.

GONERIL You see how full of changes his age is. The ob-
servation we have made of it hath not been little. He

---

268 *jewels* i.e. things held precious (cf. l. 259); *washed* tear-washed 270
like a sister i.e. with sisterly loyalty 271 *as . . . named* by their true names
272 *professèd* i.e. love-professing 274 *prefer* promote 278 *alms* small
offerings 279 *worth . . . wanted* i.e. deserving no affection since you have
shown no affection 280 *plighted* pleated, enfolded 281 *Who . . . derides*
i.e. time at first conceals faults, then exposes them to shame

always loved our sister most, and with what poor judgment he hath now cast her off appears too grossly. 291

REGAN 'Tis the infirmity of his age; yet he hath ever but
slenderly known himself. 293

GONERIL The best and soundest of his time hath been but 294
rash; then must we look from his age to receive not alone
the imperfections of long-ingraffed condition, but there- 296
withal the unruly waywardness that infirm and choleric
years bring with them.

REGAN Such unconstant starts are we like to have from 299
him as this of Kent's banishment.

GONERIL There is further compliment of leave-taking 301
between France and him. Pray you let us hit together; if 302
our father carry authority with such disposition as he
bears, this last surrender of his will but offend us. 304

REGAN We shall further think of it.

GONERIL We must do something, and i' th' heat. *Exeunt.* 306

*

Enter Bastard [Edmund, solus, with a letter]. I, ii

EDMUND
  Thou, Nature, art my goddess; to thy law 1
  My services are bound. Wherefore should I
  Stand in the plague of custom, and permit 3
  The curiosity of nations to deprive me, 4
  For that I am some twelve or fourteen moonshines 5

---

291 *grossly* crudely conspicuous 293 *known himself* i.e. been aware of what
he truly is 294 *of his time* period of his past life 296 *long-ingraffed* in-
grown, chronic; *therewithal* along with that 299 *unconstant starts* im-
pulsive moves 301 *compliment* formality 302 *hit* agree 304 *surrender* i.e.
yielding up of authority; *offend* harm 306 *i' th' heat* i.e. while the iron is hot
I, ii Within the Earl of Gloucester's castle 1 *Nature* i.e. the material and
mechanistic as distinct from the spiritual and heaven-ordained 3 *Stand
. . . custom* submit to the affliction of convention 4 *curiosity* nice distinctions 5 *For that* because; *moonshines* months

6   Lag of a brother ? Why bastard ? Wherefore base,
7   When my dimensions are as well compact,
8   My mind as generous, and my shape as true,
9   As honest madam's issue ? Why brand they us
     With base ? with baseness ? Bastardy base ? Base ?
11   Who, in the lusty stealth of nature, take
12   More composition and fierce quality
     Than doth, within a dull, stale, tirèd bed,
14   Go to th' creating a whole tribe of fops
15   Got 'tween asleep and wake ? Well then,
     Legitimate Edgar, I must have your land.
     Our father's love is to the bastard Edmund
     As to th' legitimate. Fine word, 'legitimate.'
     Well, my legitimate, if this letter speed,
20   And my invention thrive, Edmund the base
     Shall top th' legitimate. I grow, I prosper.
     Now, gods, stand up for bastards.
          Enter Gloucester.

GLOUCESTER
     Kent banished thus ? and France in choler parted ?
24   And the King gone to-night ? prescribed his pow'r ?
25   Confined to exhibition ? All this done
26   Upon the gad ? – Edmund, how now ? What news ?

EDMUND
     So please your lordship, none.

GLOUCESTER
28   Why so earnestly seek you to put up that letter ?

EDMUND
     I know no news, my lord.

GLOUCESTER
     What paper were you reading ?

EDMUND Nothing, my lord.

---

6 *Lag of* behind (in age) 7 *compact* fitted, matched 8 *generous* befitting the high-born 9 *honest* chaste 11 *lusty . . . nature* secrecy of natural lust 12 *composition* completeness of constitution, robustness; *fierce* mettlesome, thoroughbred 14 *fops* fools 15 *Got* begotten 20 *invention thrive* plot succeed 24 *prescribed* limited 25 *exhibition* an allowance, a pension 26 *gad* spur 28 *put up* put away

GLOUCESTER No? What needed then that terrible dispatch of it into your pocket? The quality of nothing
hath not such need to hide itself. Let's see. Come, if it
be nothing, I shall not need spectacles.

EDMUND I beseech you, sir, pardon me. It is a letter from
my brother that I have not all o'er-read; and for so much
as I have perused, I find it not fit for your o'erlooking.   38

GLOUCESTER Give me the letter, sir.

EDMUND I shall offend, either to detain or give it. The
contents, as in part I understand them, are to blame.   41

GLOUCESTER Let's see, let's see.

EDMUND I hope, for my brother's justification, he wrote
this but as an essay or taste of my virtue.   44

GLOUCESTER (reads) 'This policy and reverence of age   45
makes the world bitter to the best of our times; keeps our   46
fortunes from us till our oldness cannot relish them. I
begin to find an idle and fond bondage in the oppression   48
of aged tyranny, who sways, not as it hath power, but as   49
it is suffered. Come to me, that of this I may speak more.   50
If our father would sleep till I waked him, you should
enjoy half his revenue for ever, and live the beloved of   52
your brother,   Edgar.'

Hum! Conspiracy? 'Sleep till I waked him, you should
enjoy half his revenue.' My son Edgar! Had he a hand to
write this? A heart and brain to breed it in? When came
you to this? Who brought it?   57

EDMUND It was not brought me, my lord; there's the
cunning of it. I found it thrown in at the casement of my   59
closet.   60

GLOUCESTER You know the character to be your   61
brother's?

38 *o'erlooking* examination   41 *to blame* blameworthy   44 *essay* trial; *taste*
test   45 *policy and reverence* policy of reverencing   46 *the best of our times*
our best years   48 *idle, fond* foolish (synonyms)   49 *who sways* which rules
50 *suffered* allowed   52 *revenue* income   57 *to this* upon this   59 *casement*
window   60 *closet* room   61 *character* handwriting

62 EDMUND If the matter were good, my lord, I durst swear
63 it were his; but in respect of that, I would fain think it
were not.

GLOUCESTER It is his.

EDMUND It is his hand, my lord; but I hope his heart is
not in the contents.

68 GLOUCESTER Has he never before sounded you in this
business?

EDMUND Never, my lord. But I have heard him oft main-
71 tain it to be fit that, sons at perfect age, and fathers
declined, the father should be as ward to the son, and
the son manage his revenue.

GLOUCESTER O villain, villain! His very opinion in the
letter. Abhorred villain, unnatural, detested, brutish
76 villain; worse than brutish! Go, sirrah, seek him. I'll
apprehend him. Abominable villain! Where is he?

EDMUND I do not well know, my lord. If it shall please
you to suspend your indignation against my brother till
you can derive from him better testimony of his intent,
81 you should run a certain course; where, if you violently
proceed against him, mistaking his purpose, it would
make a great gap in your own honor and shake in pieces
the heart of his obedience. I dare pawn down my life for
85 him that he hath writ this to feel my affection to your
86 honor, and to no other pretense of danger.

GLOUCESTER Think you so?

88 EDMUND If your honor judge it meet, I will place you
89 where you shall hear us confer of this and by an auri-
cular assurance have your satisfaction, and that without
any further delay than this very evening.

GLOUCESTER He cannot be such a monster.

---

62 *matter* contents   63 *in respect of that* i.e. considering what those contents
are; *fain* prefer to   68 *sounded you* sounded you out   71 *perfect age* prime
of life   76 *sirrah* sir (familiar, or contemptuous, form)   81 *run . . . course*
i.e. know where you are going   85 *feel* feel out, test; *affection* attachment,
loyalty   86 *pretense of danger* dangerous intention   88 *judge it meet*
consider it fitting   89–90 *by . . . assurance* i.e. by the proof of your own ears

[EDMUND Nor is not, sure.

GLOUCESTER To his father, that so tenderly and entirely
loves him. Heaven and earth!] Edmund, seek him out;
wind me into him, I pray you; frame the business after 96
your own wisdom I would unstate myself to be in a due 97
resolution.

EDMUND I will seek him, sir, presently; convey the busi- 99
ness as I shall find means, and acquaint you withal. 100

GLOUCESTER These late eclipses in the sun and moon 101
portend no good to us. Though the wisdom of nature can 102
reason it thus and thus, yet nature finds itself scourged by 103
the sequent effects. Love cools, friendship falls off, 104
brothers divide. In cities, mutinies; in countries, dis- 105
cord; in palaces, treason; and the bond cracked 'twixt
son and father. This villain of mine comes under the pre- 107
diction, there's son against father; the King falls from
bias of nature, there's father against child. We have seen 109
the best of our time. Machinations, hollowness, treachery, and all ruinous disorders follow us disquietly to our
graves. Find out this villain, Edmund; it shall lose thee 112
nothing; do it carefully. And the noble and true-hearted
Kent banished; his offense, honesty. 'Tis strange. *Exit*.

EDMUND This is the excellent foppery of the world, that 115
when we are sick in fortune, often the surfeits of our own 116
behavior, we make guilty of our disasters the sun, the
moon, and stars; as if we were villains on necessity; fools
by heavenly compulsion; knaves, thieves, and treachers 119
by spherical predominance; drunkards, liars, and adul- 120

96 *wind me* worm; *frame* plan   97–98 *unstate . . . resolution* i.e. give everything to know for certain   99 *presently* at once; *convey* conduct   100 *withal*
therewith   101 *late* recent   102 *wisdom of nature* natural lore, science
102–04 *can . . . effects* i.e. can supply explanations, yet punitive upheavals in
nature (such as earthquakes) follow   103 *scourged* whipped   104 *sequent*
following   105 *mutinies* rebellions   107 *comes . . . prediction* i.e. is included
among these ill-omened things   109 *bias of nature* natural tendency
112–13 *lose thee nothing* i.e. you will not lose by it   115 *foppery* foolishness
116 *we are sick . . . surfeits* i.e. our fortunes grow sickly, often from the
excesses   119 *treachers* traitors   120 *spherical predominance* i.e. ascen-
dancy, or rule, of a particular sphere

terers by an enforced obedience of planetary influence;
and all that we are evil in, by a divine thrusting on. An
123 admirable evasion of whoremaster man, to lay his goatish
124 disposition on the charge of a star. My father compoun-
125 ded with my mother under the Dragon's Tail, and my
126 nativity was under Ursa Major, so that it follows I am
rough and lecherous. Fut! I should have been that I am,
had the maidenliest star in the firmament twinkled on
my bastardizing. Edgar –
        Enter Edgar.
130 and pat he comes, like the catastrophe of the old comedy.
131 My cue is villainous melancholy, with a sigh like Tom o'
Bedlam. – O, these eclipses do portend these divisions.
Fa, sol, la, mi.

EDGAR How now, brother Edmund; what serious con-
templation are you in?

EDMUND I am thinking, brother, of a prediction I read
this other day, what should follow these eclipses.

EDGAR Do you busy yourself with that?

139 EDMUND I promise you, the effects he writes of succeed
140 unhappily: [as of unnaturalness between the child and
the parent; death, dearth, dissolutions of ancient ami-
ties; divisions in state, menaces and maledictions
143 against king and nobles; needless diffidences, banish-
144 ment of friends, dissipation of cohorts, nuptial breaches,
and I know not what.

146 EDGAR How long have you been a sectary astronomical?

EDMUND Come, come,] when saw you my father last?

EDGAR The night gone by.

---

123 *goatish* lecherous   **124** *compounded* (1) came to terms, (2) created
125, 126 *Dragon's Tail, Ursa Major* (constellations, cited because of the
suggestiveness of their names)   **126** *nativity* birthday   **130** *catastrophe*
conclusion   **131–32** *Tom o' Bedlam* (a type of beggar, mad or pretending
to be, so named from the London madhouse, Bethlehem or 'Bedlam'
Hospital)   **139–40** *succeed unhappily* unluckily follow   **140** *unnaturalness*
unkindness, enmity   **143** *diffidences* instances of distrust   **144** *dissipation
of cohorts* melting away of supporters   **146** *sectary astronomical* of the
astrological sect

EDMUND Spake you with him?

EDGAR Ay, two hours together.

EDMUND Parted you in good terms? Found you no displeasure in him by word nor countenance?   152

EDGAR None at all.

EDMUND Bethink yourself wherein you may have offended him; and at my entreaty forbear his presence until
some little time hath qualified the heat of his displeasure,   156
which at this instant so rageth in him that with the mis-   157
chief of your person it would scarcely allay.   158

EDGAR Some villain hath done me wrong.

EDMUND That's my fear. I pray you have a continent for-   160
bearance till the speed of his rage goes slower; and, as I
say, retire with me to my lodging, from whence I will
fitly bring you to hear my lord speak. Pray ye, go;   163
there's my key. If you do stir abroad, go armed.

EDGAR Armed, brother?

EDMUND Brother, I advise you to the best. Go armed. I
am no honest man if there be any good meaning toward
you. I have told you what I have seen and heard; but
faintly, nothing like the image and horror of it. Pray   169
you, away.

EDGAR Shall I hear from you anon?   170

EDMUND I do serve you in this business.   *Exit [Edgar].*
A credulous father, and a brother noble,
Whose nature is so far from doing harms
That he suspects none; on whose foolish honesty
My practices ride easy. I see the business.   175
Let me, if not by birth, have lands by wit;   176
All with me's meet that I can fashion fit.   *Exit.* 177

*

152 *countenance* expression, look   156 *qualified* moderated   157 *mischief*
injury   158 *allay* be appeased   160 *continent forbearance* cautious in-
accessibility   163 *fitly* conveniently   169 *image and horror* horrible true
picture   170 *anon* soon   175 *practices* plots   176 *wit* intelligence   177
meet proper, acceptable; *fashion fit* i.e. rig up, shape to the purpose

I, iii   *Enter Goneril and Steward [Oswald].*

GONERIL
  Did my father strike my gentleman for chiding of his
       fool?

OSWALD Ay, madam.

GONERIL
  By day and night he wrongs me. Every hour
4 He flashes into one gross crime or other
  That sets us all at odds. I'll not endure it.
6 His knights grow riotous, and himself upbraids us
  On every trifle. When he returns from hunting,
  I will not speak with him. Say I am sick.
9 If you come slack of former services,
10 You shall do well; the fault of it I'll answer.
       [Horns within.]

OSWALD He's coming, madam; I hear him.

GONERIL
  Put on what weary negligence you please,
13 You and your fellows. I'd have it come to question.
14 If he distaste it, let him to my sister,
  Whose mind and mine I know in that are one,
16 [Not to be overruled. Idle old man,
  That still would manage those authorities
  That he hath given away. Now, by my life,
  Old fools are babes again, and must be used
20 With checks as flatteries, when they are seen abused.]
  Remember what I have said.

OSWALD   Well, madam.

GONERIL
  And let his knights have colder looks among you.
  What grows of it, no matter; advise your fellows so.

I, iii Within the Duke of Albany's palace **4** *crime* offense **6** *riotous*
boisterous **9** *come . . . services* i.e. serve him less well than formerly
10 *answer* answer for **13** *question* i.e. open issue, a thing discussed
14 *distaste* dislike **16** *Idle* foolish **20** *checks . . . abused* restraints in
place of cajolery when they (the old men) are seen to be deceived (about
their true state)

[I would breed from hence occasions, and I shall,   24
That I may speak.] I'll write straight to my sister
To hold my course. Prepare for dinner.   *Exeunt.*
          Enter Kent [disguised].   I, iv

KENT

If but as well I other accents borrow
That can my speech defuse, my good intent   2
May carry through itself to that full issue   3
For which I razed my likeness. Now, banished Kent,   4
If thou canst serve where thou dost stand condemned,
So may it come thy master whom thou lov'st
Shall find thee full of labors.
          Horns within. Enter Lear, [Knight,] and Attendants.

LEAR Let me not stay a jot for dinner; go get it ready.   8
[Exit an Attendant.] How now, what art thou?

KENT A man, sir.

LEAR What dost thou profess? What wouldst thou with   11
us?

KENT I do profess to be no less than I seem, to serve him 12
truly that will put me in trust, to love him that is honest,
to converse with him that is wise and says little, to fear 14
judgment, to fight when I cannot choose, and to eat no   15
fish.

LEAR What art thou?

KENT A very honest-hearted fellow, and as poor as the
King.

LEAR If thou be'st as poor for a subject as he's for a king,
thou art poor enough. What wouldst thou?

KENT Service.

LEAR Who wouldst thou serve?

KENT You.

LEAR Dost thou know me, fellow?

24–25 *breed . . . speak* i.e. make an issue of it so that I may speak
I, iv 2 *defuse* disorder, disguise 3 *full issue* perfect result 4 *razed
my likeness* erased my natural appearance 8 *stay* wait 11 *profess* do,
work at (with pun following) 12 *profess* claim 14 *converse* associate
15 *judgment* i.e. God's judgment 15–16 *eat no fish* be a Protestant (ana-
chronism)(?), avoid unmanly diet(?)

KENT No, sir, but you have that in your countenance
27   which I would fain call master.

LEAR What's that?

KENT Authority.

LEAR What services canst thou do?

31 KENT I can keep honest counsel, ride, run, mar a curious
      tale in telling it, and deliver a plain message bluntly.
      That which ordinary men are fit for I am qualified in,
      and the best of me is diligence.

LEAR How old art thou?

KENT Not so young, sir, to love a woman for singing, nor
      so old to dote on her for anything. I have years on my
      back forty-eight.

LEAR Follow me; thou shalt serve me. If I like thee no
      worse after dinner, I will not part from thee yet. Dinner,
41   ho, dinner! Where's my knave? my fool? Go you and
      call my fool hither.   [*Exit an Attendant.*]
           Enter Steward [Oswald].
      You, you, sirrah, where's my daughter?

OSWALD So please you –   *Exit.*

45 LEAR What says the fellow there? Call the clotpoll back.
      [*Exit Knight.*] Where's my fool? Ho, I think the world's
      asleep. [*Enter Knight.*] How now? Where's that
      mongrel?

KNIGHT He says, my lord, your daughter is not well.

LEAR Why came not the slave back to me when I called
      him?

KNIGHT Sir, he answered me in the roundest manner, he
      would not.

LEAR He would not?

KNIGHT My lord, I know not what the matter is; but to
56   my judgment your Highness is not entertained with
      that ceremonious affection as you were wont. There's a

---

27 *fain* like to   31 *keep honest counsel* keep counsel honestly, i.e. respect con-
fidences; *curious* elaborate, embroidered (as contrasted with *plain*)   41
knave boy   45 *clotpoll* clodpoll, dolt   56 *entertained* rendered hospitality

great abatement of kindness appears as well in the general dependants as in the Duke himself also and your daughter.

LEAR Ha? Say'st thou so?

KNIGHT I beseech you pardon me, my lord, if I be mistaken; for my duty cannot be silent when I think your Highness wronged.

LEAR Thou but rememb'rest me of mine own conception. 64
I have perceived a most faint neglect of late, which I have 65
rather blamed as mine own jealous curiosity than as a 66
very pretense and purpose of unkindness. I will look 67
further into't. But where's my fool? I have not seen him this two days.

KNIGHT Since my young lady's going into France, sir, the fool hath much pined away.

LEAR No more of that; I have noted it well. Go you and tell my daughter I would speak with her. *[Exit Knight.]*
Go you, call hither my fool.   *[Exit an Attendant.]*
     Enter Steward [Oswald].

O, you, sir, you! Come you hither, sir. Who am I, sir?

OSWALD My lady's father.

LEAR 'My lady's father'? My lord's knave, you whoreson dog, you slave, you cur!

OSWALD I am none of these, my lord; I beseech your pardon.

LEAR Do you bandy looks with me, you rascal?   80
     [Strikes him.]

OSWALD I'll not be strucken, my lord.   81

KENT Nor tripped neither, you base football player.   82
     [Trips up his heels.]

LEAR I thank thee, fellow. Thou serv'st me, and I'll love thee.

---

64 *rememb'rest* remind   65 *faint neglect* i.e. the *weary negligence* of I, iii, 12
66 *jealous curiosity* i.e. suspicious concern about trifles   67 *very pretense* true intention   80 *bandy* volley, exchange   81 *strucken* struck   82 *football* (an impromptu street and field game, held in low esteem)

85 KENT Come, sir, arise, away. I'll teach you differences.
Away, away. If you will measure your lubber's length
87 again, tarry; but away. Go to! Have you wisdom? So.
[Pushes him out.]

88 LEAR Now, my friendly knave, I thank thee. There's earnest of thy service.
[Gives money.] Enter Fool.

90 FOOL Let me hire him too. Here's my coxcomb.
[Offers Kent his cap.]

LEAR How now, my pretty knave? How dost thou?

FOOL Sirrah, you were best take my coxcomb.

KENT Why, fool?

FOOL Why? For taking one's part that's out of favor. Nay,
95 an thou canst not smile as the wind sits, thou'lt catch
cold shortly. There, take my coxcomb. Why, this fellow
97 has banished two on's daughters, and did the third a
blessing against his will. If thou follow him, thou must
99 needs wear my coxcomb. – How now, nuncle? Would I
had two coxcombs and two daughters.

LEAR Why, my boy?

FOOL If I gave them all my living, I'ld keep my coxcombs
myself. There's mine; beg another of thy daughters.

LEAR Take heed, sirrah – the whip.

FOOL Truth's a dog must to kennel; he must be whipped
106 out, when the Lady Brach may stand by th' fire and
stink.

108 LEAR A pestilent gall to me.

FOOL Sirrah, I'll teach thee a speech.

LEAR Do.

FOOL Mark it, nuncle.

> Have more than thou showest,
> Speak less than thou knowest,

---

85 *differences* distinctions in rank   87 *Go to!* . . . *wisdom* i.e. Get along! Do
you know what's good for you?   88 *earnest* part payment   90 *coxcomb* (cap
of the professional fool, topped with an imitation comb)   95 *smile* . . . *sits* i.e.
adapt yourself to prevailing forces   97 *banished* i.e. provided the means for
them to become alien to him   99 *nuncle* mine uncle   106 *Brach* hound
bitch   108 *gall* sore, source of irritation

Lend less than thou owest,   114
Ride more than thou goest,   115
Learn more than thou trowest,   116
Set less than thou throwest;   117
Leave thy drink and thy whore,
And keep in-a-door,
And thou shalt have more   120
Than two tens to a score.

KENT This is nothing, fool.

FOOL Then 'tis like the breath of an unfee'd lawyer – you 123
land comes to; he will not believe a fool.
gave me nothing for't. Can you make no use of nothing,
nuncle?

LEAR Why, no, boy. Nothing can be made out of nothing.

FOOL *[to Kent]* Prithee tell him, so much the rent of his 127
land comes to; he will not believe a fool.

LEAR A bitter fool.

FOOL Dost thou know the difference, my boy, between a
bitter fool and a sweet one?   131

LEAR No, lad; teach me.

FOOL   [That lord that counselled thee
                  To give away thy land,
               Come place him here by me –
                  Do thou for him stand.   136
               The sweet and bitter fool
                  Will presently appear;
               The one in motley here,
                  The other found out there.   140

LEAR Dost thou call me fool, boy?

FOOL All thy other titles thou hast given away; that thou
wast born with.

---

114 *owest* borrow (?), own, keep (?)   115 *goest* walk   116 *Learn* hear,
listen to; *trowest* believe   117 *Set . . . throwest* stake less than you throw for
(i.e. play for odds)   120–21 *have . . . score* i.e. do better than break even
123 *breath* voice, counsel (reliable only when paid for)   127–28 *rent . . .
land* (nothing, since he has no land)   131 *bitter, sweet* satirical, non-satirical
136 *Do . . . stand* (the Fool thus identifying Lear as his own foolish
counsellor)   140 *found out* revealed (since Lear is the *born* fool as distinct
from himself, the fool in *motley*, professionally satirical)

KENT This is not altogether fool, my lord.

145 FOOL No, faith; lords and great men will not let me. If I
had a monopoly out, they would have part on't. And
ladies too, they will not let me have all the fool to my-
148 self; they'll be snatching.] Nuncle, give me an egg, and
I'll give thee two crowns.

LEAR What two crowns shall they be?

FOOL Why, after I have cut the egg i' th' middle and eat
up the meat, the two crowns of the egg. When thou
clovest thy crown i' th' middle and gav'st away both
154 parts, thou bor'st thine ass on thy back o'er the dirt.
Thou hadst little wit in thy bald crown when thou
156 gav'st thy golden one away. If I speak like myself in
157 this, let him be whipped that first finds it so.
158 [Sings]   Fools had ne'er less grace in a year,
159   For wise men are grown foppish,
160   And know not how their wits to wear,
                       Their manners are so apish.

LEAR When were you wont to be so full of songs, sirrah?

163 FOOL I have used it, nuncle, e'er since thou mad'st thy
daughters thy mothers; for when thou gav'st them the
rod, and put'st down thine own breeches,
      [Sings]   Then they for sudden joy did weep,
                    And I for sorrow sung,
168   That such a king should play bo-peep
                    And go the fools among.
Prithee, nuncle, keep a schoolmaster that can teach thy
fool to lie. I would fain learn to lie.

172 LEAR An you lie, sirrah, we'll have you whipped.

FOOL I marvel what kin thou and thy daughters are.

---

145 *let me* (i.e. be all fool, since they seek a share of folly)   **148** *snatching*
(like greedy courtiers seeking shares in royal patents of monopoly)   **154**
bor'st . . . dirt (thus foolishly reversing normal behavior)   **156** *like myself*
i.e. like a fool   **157** *let . . . so* i.e. let him be whipped (as a fool) who mis-
takes this truth as my typical folly   **158** *grace . . . year* favor at any time
159 *foppish* foolish   **160** *their wits to wear* i.e. to use their intelligence
163 *used* practiced   **168** *play bo-peep* i.e. act like a child   **172** *An* if

They'll have me whipped for speaking true; thou'lt have me whipped for lying; and sometimes I am whipped for holding my peace. I had rather be any kind o' thing than a fool, and yet I would not be thee, nuncle: thou hast pared thy wit o' both sides and left nothing i' th' middle.   178 Here comes one o' the parings.

Enter Goneril.

LEAR How now, daughter? What makes that frontlet on?   180 You are too much of late i' th' frown.

FOOL Thou wast a pretty fellow when thou hadst no need to care for her frowning. Now thou art an O without a   183 figure. I am better than thou art now: I am a fool, thou art nothing. *[to Goneril]* Yes, forsooth, I will hold my tongue. So your face bids me, though you say nothing. Mum, mum,

>   He that keeps nor crust nor crum,   188
>   Weary of all, shall want some. –   189

[Points at Lear.]

That's a shealed peascod.   190

GONERIL

Not only, sir, this your all-licensed fool,   191
But other of your insolent retinue
Do hourly carp and quarrel, breaking forth   193
In rank and not-to-be-endurèd riots. Sir,
I had thought by making this well known unto you
To have found a safe redress, but now grow fearful,   196
By what yourself too late have spoke and done,
That you protect this course, and put it on   198
By your allowance; which if you should, the fault   199
Would not 'scape censure, nor the redresses sleep,   200
Which, in the tender of a wholesome weal,   201

---

178 *pared . . . middle* i.e. completely disposed of your wits (in disposing of your power)   **180** *frontlet* band worn across the brow; hence, frown   **183–84** *O . . . figure* cipher without a digit to give it value   **188** *crum* soft bread within the crust   **189** *want* need   **190** *shealed* shelled, empty; *peascod* pea-pod   **191** *all-licensed* all privileged   **193** *carp* complain   **196** *safe* sure   **198** *put it on* instigate it   **199** *allowance* approval   **200** *redresses sleep* correction lie dormant   **201** *tender of* care for; *weal* state

202   Might in their working do you that offense,
       Which else were shame, that then necessity
       Will call discreet proceeding.

    FOOL   For you know, nuncle,

206   The hedge-sparrow fed the cuckoo so long
207   That it's had it head bit off by it young.
208   So out went the candle, and we were left darkling.

    LEAR   Are you our daughter?

    GONERIL
       I would you would make use of your good wisdom
211   (Whereof I know you are fraught) and put away
212   These dispositions which of late transport you
       From what you rightly are.

    FOOL   May not an ass know when the cart draws the horse?
215   Whoop, Jug, I love thee!

    LEAR
       Does any here know me? This is not Lear.
       Does Lear walk thus? speak thus? Where are his eyes?
218   Either his notion weakens, his discernings
219   Are lethargied – Ha! Waking? 'Tis not so.
       Who is it that can tell me who I am?

    FOOL   Lear's shadow.

    [LEAR
222   I would learn that; for, by the marks of sovereignty,
       Knowledge, and reason, I should be false persuaded
       I had daughters.

    FOOL   Which they will make an obedient father.]

    LEAR   Your name, fair gentlewoman?

202–04 *Might . . . proceeding* in their operation might be considered humiliating to you but, under the circumstances, are merely prudent **206** *cuckoo* (an image suggesting illegitimacy as well as voraciousness, since the cuckoo lays its eggs in the nests of other birds) **207** *it* its **208** *darkling* in the dark (like the dead hedge-sparrow and the threatened Lear) **211** *fraught* freighted, laden **212** *dispositions* moods **215** *Jug* Joan (evidently part of some catch-phrase) **218** *notion* understanding **219** *Ha! Waking* i.e. so I am really awake (presumably accompanied by the 'business' of pinching himself) **222** *marks of sovereignty* evidences that I am King (and hence the father of the princesses)

GONERIL

This admiration, sir, is much o' th' savor   227
Of other your new pranks. I do beseech you
To understand my purposes aright.
As you are old and reverend, should be wise.
Here do you keep a hundred knights and squires,
Men so disordered, so deboshed and bold   232
That this our court, infected with their manners,
Shows like a riotous inn. Epicurism and lust   234
Makes it more like a tavern or a brothel
Than a graced palace. The shame itself doth speak   236
For instant remedy. Be then desired
By her that else will take the thing she begs
A little to disquantity your train,   239
And the remainders that shall still depend   240
To be such men as may besort your age,   241
Which know themselves, and you.   242

LEAR   Darkness and devils!

Saddle my horses; call my train together.
Degenerate bastard, I'll not trouble thee: 244
Yet have I left a daughter.

GONERIL

You strike my people, and your disordered rabble
Make servants of their betters.

    Enter Albany.

LEAR

Woe that too late repents. – [O, sir, are you come?]
Is it your will? Speak, sir. – Prepare my horses.
Ingratitude! thou marble-hearted fiend,
More hideous when thou show'st thee in a child
Than the sea-monster.

ALBANY   Pray, sir, be patient.

---

227 *admiration* air of wonderment   **232** *deboshed* debauched   **234** *Epicurism* loose living   **236** *graced* honored; *shame* disgrace   **239** *disquantity your train* reduce the size of your retinue   **240** *depend* be attached   **241** *besort* befit   **242** *Which know* i.e. who are aware of the status of   **244** *Degenerate* unnatural, fallen away from kind

LEAR

253 Detested kite, thou liest.

254 My train are men of choice and rarest parts,
That all particulars of duty know

256 And in the most exact regard support
257 The worships of their name. O most small fault,
How ugly didst thou in Cordelia show!

259 Which, like an engine, wrenched my frame of nature
From the fixed place; drew from my heart all love

261 And added to the gall. O Lear, Lear, Lear!
Beat at this gate that let thy folly in
     [Strikes his head.]
And thy dear judgment out. Go, go, my people.

ALBANY

My lord, I am guiltless, as I am ignorant
Of what hath moved you.

LEAR   It may be so, my lord.
Hear, Nature, hear; dear goddess, hear:
Suspend thy purpose if thou didst intend
To make this creature fruitful.
Into her womb convey sterility,
Dry up in her the organs of increase,

271 And from her derogate body never spring
272 A babe to honor her. If she must teem,
273 Create her child of spleen, that it may live
274 And be a thwart disnatured torment to her.
Let it stamp wrinkles in her brow of youth,

276 With cadent tears fret channels in her cheeks,
277 Turn all her mother's pains and benefits
To laughter and contempt, that she may feel

---

253 *Detested kite* detestable bird of prey   254 *parts* accomplishments
256 *exact regard* careful attention, punctiliousness   257 *worships* honor
259 *engine* destructive contrivance of war   259–60 *wrenched . . . place* set
askew my natural structure, distorted my normal self   261 *gall* bitterness
271 *derogate* degraded   272 *teem* increase   273 *spleen* ill-humor, spite-
fulness   274 *thwart disnatured* perverse unnatural   276 *cadent* falling;
fret wear   277 *pains and benefits* care and offerings

How sharper than a serpent's tooth it is
To have a thankless child. Away, away!   *Exit.*

ALBANY
Now, gods that we adore, whereof comes this?

GONERIL
Never afflict yourself to know more of it,
But let his disposition have that scope   283
As dotage gives it.
        Enter Lear.

LEAR
What, fifty of my followers at a clap?
Within a fortnight?

ALBANY   What's the matter, sir?

LEAR
I'll tell thee. *[to Goneril]* Life and death, I am ashamed
That thou hast power to shake my manhood thus!
That these hot tears, which break from me perforce,   289
Should make thee worth them. Blasts and fogs upon
    thee!
Th' untented woundings of a father's curse   291
Pierce every sense about thee! Old fond eyes,   292
Beweep this cause again I'll pluck ye out   293
And cast you, with the waters that you loose,   294
To temper clay. [Yea, is it come to this?]   295
Ha! Let it be so. I have another daughter,
Who I am sure is kind and comfortable.   297
When she shall hear this of thee, with her nails
She'll flay thy wolvish visage. Thou shalt find
That I'll resume the shape which thou dost think   300
I have cast off for ever.
        Exit [Lear with Kent and Attendants].

GONERIL   Do you mark that?

---

283 *disposition* mood   289 *perforce* by force, against my will   291 *untented* untentable, too deep for treatment by a probe   292 *sense about* faculty possessed by; *fond* foolish   293 *Beweep this cause* if you weep over this matter   294 *loose* let loose   295 *temper* soften   297 *comfortable* ready to comfort   300 *shape* i.e. role of authority

ALBANY

302   I cannot be so partial, Goneril,
      To the great love I bear you –

GONERIL

      Pray you, content. – What, Oswald, ho !
      [To Fool]
      You, sir, more knave than fool, after your master !

306 FOOL Nuncle Lear, nuncle Lear, tarry. Take the fool
      with thee.

               A fox, when one has caught her,
               And such a daughter,
310   Should sure to the slaughter,
311   If my cap would buy a halter.
312   So the fool follows after.   *Exit.*

GONERIL

313   This man hath had good counsel – a hundred knights !
314   'Tis politic and safe to let him keep
315   At point a hundred knights – yes, that on every dream,
316   Each buzz, each fancy, each complaint, dislike,
      He may enguard his dotage with their pow'rs
318   And hold our lives in mercy. – Oswald, I say !

ALBANY

      Well, you may fear too far.

GONERIL   Safer than trust too far.

320   Let me still take away the harms I fear,
321   Not fear still to be taken. I know his heart.
      What he hath uttered I have writ my sister.
      If she sustain him and his hundred knights,
      When I have showed th' unfitness –

        Enter Steward [Oswald].   How now, Oswald ?
      What, have you writ that letter to my sister ?

302–03 *partial . . . To* made partial . . . by   306 *the fool* i.e. both your fool
and your folly   310 *slaughter* hanging and quartering   311, 312 *halter,
after* (pronounced 'hauter,' 'auter')   313 *good counsel* i.e. from such
company (ironic)   314 *politic* prudent   315 *At point* in arms   316 *buzz*
murmur   318 *in mercy* at his mercy   320 *still . . . harms* always eliminate
the sources of injury   321 *still . . . taken* always to be overtaken (by them)

OSWALD Ay, madam.

GONERIL

    Take you some company, and away to horse.   327

    Inform her full of my particular fear,   328

    And thereto add such reasons of your own

    As may compact it more. Get you gone,   330

    And hasten your return. [Exit Oswald.] No, no, my lord,

    This milky gentleness and course of yours,   332

    Though I condemn not, yet under pardon,

    You are much more ataskèd for want of wisdom   334

    Than praised for harmful mildness.   335

ALBANY

    How far your eyes may pierce I cannot tell;

    Striving to better, oft we mar what's well.

GONERIL Nay then –

ALBANY Well, well; th' event.   *Exeunt.* 339

*

    Enter Lear, Kent, and Fool.   I, v

LEAR Go you before to Gloucester with these letters. Acquaint my daughter no further with anything you know than comes from her demand out of the letter. If your 3 diligence be not speedy, I shall be there afore you.

KENT I will not sleep, my lord, till I have delivered your letter.   *Exit.*

FOOL If a man's brains were in's heels, were't not in danger of kibes?   8

LEAR Ay, boy.

FOOL Then I prithee be merry. Thy wit shall not go slip- 10 shod.

LEAR Ha, ha, ha.

327 *some company* an escort 328 *particular* own 330 *compact it more* substantiate it further 332 *milky . . . course* mildly gentle way 334 *ataskèd* censured, taken to task 335 *harmful mildness* mildness that proves harmful 339 *th' event* the outcome, i.e. we shall see what happens
I, v The courtyard of Albany's palace 3 *demand out of* i.e. questioning provoked by reading 8 *kibes* chilblains 10 *wit . . . slipshod* intelligence (*brains*) shall not go slippered (because of *kibes*)

12 FOOL Shalt see thy other daughter will use thee kindly;
13   for though she's as like this as a crab 's like an apple, yet I can tell what I can tell.

LEAR What canst tell, boy?

FOOL She will taste as like this as a crab does to a crab. Thou canst tell why one's nose stands i' th' middle on's face?

LEAR No.

FOOL Why, to keep one's eyes of either side 's nose, that what a man cannot smell out he may spy into.

21 LEAR I did her wrong.

FOOL Canst tell how an oyster makes his shell?

LEAR No.

FOOL Nor I neither; but I can tell why a snail has a house.

LEAR Why?

FOOL Why, to put 's head in; not to give it away to his
27 daughters, and leave his horns without a case.

28 LEAR I will forget my nature. So kind a father! – Be my horses ready?

FOOL Thy asses are gone about 'em. The reason why the
31 seven stars are no moe than seven is a pretty reason.

LEAR Because they are not eight.

FOOL Yes indeed. Thou wouldst make a good fool.

34 LEAR To take 't again perforce – Monster ingratitude!

FOOL If thou wert my fool, nuncle, I'ld have thee beaten for being old before thy time.

LEAR How's that?

FOOL Thou shouldst not have been old till thou hadst been wise.

LEAR
    O, let me not be mad, not mad, sweet heaven!

---

12 *Shalt* thou shalt; *kindly* after her kind, i.e. in the same way as this daughter 13 *crab* crab apple 21 *her* i.e. Cordelia (the first of the remarkable intimations of Lear's inner thoughts in this scene) 27 *horns* i.e. snail's horns (with pun on cuckold's horns; the legitimacy of Goneril and Regan being, figuratively, suspect throughout); *case* covering 28 *nature* i.e. fatherly instincts 31 *moe* more 34 *perforce* by force

Keep me in temper; I would not be mad!   41
    [Enter a Gentleman.]
How now, are the horses ready?

GENTLEMAN Ready, my lord.

LEAR Come, boy.

FOOL

She that's a maid now, and laughs at my departure,   45
Shall not be a maid long, unless things be cut shorter.
                        Exeunt.

                     *

   Enter Bastard [Edmund] and Curan severally.   II, i

EDMUND Save thee, Curan.   1

CURAN And you, sir. I have been with your father, and
given him notice that the Duke of Cornwall and Regan
his Duchess will be here with him this night.

EDMUND How comes that?

CURAN Nay, I know not. You have heard of the news
abroad – I mean the whispered ones, for they are yet but
ear-kissing arguments?   8

EDMUND Not I. Pray you, what are they?

CURAN Have you heard of no likely wars toward, 'twixt   10
the Dukes of Cornwall and Albany?

EDMUND Not a word.

CURAN You may do, then, in time. Fare you well, sir. *Exit.*

EDMUND

The Duke be here to-night? The better best!   14
This weaves itself perforce into my business.   15
My father hath set guard to take my brother,
And I have one thing of a queasy question   17

---

41 *in temper* properly balanced   45–46 *She . . . shorter* (an indecent gag
addressed to the audience, calculated to embarrass the maids who joined
in the laughter)
II, i The Earl of Gloucester's castle   1 *Save* God save   8 *ear-kissing
arguments* whispered topics   10 *likely* probable; *toward* impending
14 *better best* (hyperbole)   15 *perforce* of necessity (?), of its own accord (?)
17 *of . . . question* delicately balanced as to outcome, touch-and-go

18   Which I must act. Briefness and fortune, work!
       Brother, a word : descend. Brother, I say!
           Enter Edgar.
       My father watches. O sir, fly this place.
       Intelligence is given where you are hid.
       You have now the good advantage of the night.
       Have you not spoken 'gainst the Duke of Cornwall?
       He's coming hither ; now i' th' night, i' th' haste,
       And Regan with him. Have you nothing said
26   Upon his party 'gainst the Duke of Albany?
27   Advise yourself.

EDGAR   I am sure on't, not a word.

EDMUND
       I hear my father coming. Pardon me :
29   In cunning I must draw my sword upon you.
30   Draw, seem to defend yourself ; now quit you well. –
       Yield! Come before my father! Light ho, here! –
       Fly, brother. – Torches, torches! – So farewell.
                        Exit Edgar.
       Some blood drawn on me would beget opinion
       Of my more fierce endeavor.
           [Wounds his arm.]   I have seen drunkards
       Do more than this in sport. – Father, father!
       Stop, stop! No help?
           Enter Gloucester, and Servants with torches.

GLOUCESTER
       Now, Edmund, where's the villain?

EDMUND
       Here stood he in the dark, his sharp sword out,
       Mumbling of wicked charms, conjuring the moon
       To stand auspicious mistress.

GLOUCESTER   But where is he?

---

18 *Briefness and fortune* decisive speed and good luck   **26** *Upon his party* *'gainst* i.e. reflecting upon his feud against   **27** *Advise yourself* take thought; *on't* of it   **29** *In cunning* i.e. as a ruse   **30** *quit you* acquit yourself

EDMUND
Look, sir, I bleed.
GLOUCESTER   Where is the villain, Edmund?
EDMUND
Fled this way, sir, when by no means he could –
GLOUCESTER
Pursue him, ho! Go after.   *[Exeunt some Servants.]*
                    By no means what?
EDMUND
Persuade me to the murder of your lordship;
But that I told him the revenging gods
'Gainst parricides did all the thunder bend;   46
Spoke with how manifold and strong a bond
The child was bound to th' father – sir, in fine,   48
Seeing how loathly opposite I stood   49
To his unnatural purpose, in fell motion   50
With his preparèd sword he charges home
My unprovided body, latched mine arm;   52
And when he saw my best alarumed spirits   53
Bold in the quarrel's right, roused to th' encounter,   54
Or whether gasted by the noise I made,   55
Full suddenly he fled.
GLOUCESTER   Let him fly far.
Not in this land shall he remain uncaught;
And found – dispatch. The noble Duke my master,   58
My worthy arch and patron, comes to-night: 59
By his authority I will proclaim it
That he which finds him shall deserve our thanks,
Bringing the murderous coward to the stake;
He that conceals him, death.
EDMUND
When I dissuaded him from his intent

46 *bend* aim   48 *in fine* finally   49 *loathly opposite* in loathing opposition
50 *fell* deadly   52 *unprovided* undefended; *latched* lanced, pierced   53
best alarumed fully aroused   54 *Bold . . . right* confident in the justice of the
cause   55 *gasted* struck aghast   58 *dispatch* (equivalent to 'death' or
'finis')   59 *arch* superior

65   And found him pight to do it, with curst speech
66   I threatened to discover him. He replied,
67   'Thou unpossessing bastard, dost thou think,
68   If I would stand against thee, would the reposal
     Of any trust, virtue, or worth in thee
70   Make thy words faithed? No. What I should deny
     (As this I would, ay, though thou didst produce
72   My very character) I'ld turn it all
73   To thy suggestion, plot, and damnèd practice;
74   And thou must make a dullard of the world,
75   If they not thought the profits of my death
76   Were very pregnant and potential spirits
     To make thee seek it.'

77 GLOUCESTER   O strange and fast'ned villain!
78   Would he deny his letter, said he? [I never got him.]
               Tucket within.
     Hark, the Duke's trumpets. I know not why he comes.
     All ports I'll bar; the villain shall not 'scape;
     The Duke must grant me that. Besides, his picture
     I will send far and near, that all the kingdom
     May have due note of him; and of my land,
     Loyal and natural boy, I'll work the means
85   To make thee capable.
               Enter Cornwall, Regan, and Attendants.

   CORNWALL
     How now, my noble friend? Since I came hither
87   (Which I can call but now) I have heard strange news.

   REGAN
     If it be true, all vengeance comes too short

---

65 *pight* determined, set; *curst* angry   **66** *discover* expose   **67** *unpossessing* having no claim, landless   **68** *reposal* placing   **70** *faithed* believed   **72** *character* written testimony   **73** *suggestion* instigation; *practice* devices   **74** *make . . . world* i.e. consider everyone stupid   **75** *not thought* did not think   **76** *pregnant . . . spirits* teeming and powerful spirits, i.e. the devils which 'possess' him   **77** *fast'ned* confirmed   **78** *got* begot; **s.d.** *Tucket* (personal signature in trumpet notes)   **85** *capable* i.e. legitimate, able to inherit   **87** *call* i.e. say was

Which can pursue th' offender. How dost, my lord?

GLOUCESTER
O madam, my old heart is cracked, it's cracked.

REGAN
What, did my father's godson seek your life?
He whom my father named, your Edgar?

GLOUCESTER
O lady, lady, shame would have it hid.

REGAN
Was he not companion with the riotous knights
That tended upon my father?

GLOUCESTER
I know not, madam. 'Tis too bad, too bad.

EDMUND
Yes, madam, he was of that consort.   97

REGAN
No marvel then though he were ill affected.   98
'Tis they have put him on the old man's death,   99
To have th' expense and waste of his revenues.   100
I have this present evening from my sister
Been well informed of them, and with such cautions
That, if they come to sojourn at my house,
I'll not be there.

CORNWALL   Nor I, assure thee, Regan.
Edmund, I hear that you have shown your father
A childlike office.   106

EDMUND   It was my duty, sir.

GLOUCESTER
He did bewray his practice, and received   107
This hurt you see, striving to apprehend him.

CORNWALL
Is he pursued?

GLOUCESTER   Ay, my good lord.

---

97 *consort* company, set   98 *affected* disposed   99 *put* set   100 *expense and waste* wasteful expenditure   106 *childlike* filial   107 *bewray his practice* expose his plot

CORNWALL
If he be taken, he shall never more
111   Be feared of doing harm. Make your own purpose,
How in my strength you please. For you, Edmund,
113   Whose virtue and obedience doth this instant
So much commend itself, you shall be ours.
Natures of such deep trust we shall much need;
You we first seize on.

EDMUND   I shall serve you, sir,
Truly, however else.

GLOUCESTER   For him I thank your Grace.

CORNWALL
You know not why we came to visit you?

REGAN
Thus out of season, threading dark-eyed night.
120   Occasions, noble Gloucester, of some prize,
Wherein we must have use of your advice.
Our father he hath writ, so hath our sister,
123   Of differences, which I best thought it fit
124   To answer from our home. The several messengers
125   From hence attend dispatch. Our good old friend,
126   Lay comforts to your bosom, and bestow
127   Your needful counsel to our businesses,
128   Which craves the instant use.

GLOUCESTER   I serve you, madam.
Your Graces are right welcome.   *Exeunt. Flourish.*

*

111 *of doing* lest he do   111–12 *Make . . . please* i.e. accomplish your purpose, making free use of my powers   113 *virtue and obedience* virtuous
obedience   120 *prize* price, importance   123 *differences* quarrels; *which*
(refers, indefinitely, to the whole situation)   124 *answer . . . home* cope with
away from home (where she need not receive Lear)   125 *attend dispatch*
i.e. await settlement of the business   126 *Lay . . . bosom* be consoled (about
your own trouble)   127 *needful* needed   128 *craves . . . use* requires im-
mediate transaction (?), requires use of your counsel (?)

Enter Kent and Steward [Oswald], severally. **II, ii**

OSWALD Good dawning to thee, friend. Art of this house ? 1

KENT Ay.

OSWALD Where may we set our horses ?

KENT I' th' mire.

OSWALD Prithee, if thou lov'st me, tell me.

KENT I love thee not.

OSWALD Why then, I care not for thee.

KENT If I had thee in Lipsbury Pinfold, I would make 8
thee care for me.

OSWALD Why dost thou use me thus ? I know thee not.

KENT Fellow, I know thee.

OSWALD What dost thou know me for ?

KENT A knave, a rascal, an eater of broken meats ; a base, 13
proud, shallow, beggarly, three-suited, hundred-pound, 14
filthy worsted-stocking knave ; a lily-livered, action- 15
taking, whoreson, glass-gazing, superserviceable, finical 16
rogue ; one-trunk-inheriting slave ; one that wouldst be a 17
bawd in way of good service, and art nothing but the
composition of a knave, beggar, coward, pander, and the 19
son and heir of a mongrel bitch ; one whom I will beat
into clamorous whining if thou deny'st the least syllable
of thy addition. 22

OSWALD Why, what a monstrous fellow art thou, thus to
rail on one that is neither known of thee nor knows thee !

KENT What a brazen-faced varlet art thou to deny thou
knowest me ! Is it two days ago since I tripped up thy
heels and beat thee before the King ? *[Draws his sword.]*

II, ii Before Gloucester's castle **1** *dawning* (perhaps indicating that it is too early for 'good morning'); *Art . . . house* i.e. do you belong to this household **8** *Lipsbury Pinfold* i.e. between the teeth (cant term: 'pen in the region of the lips') **13** *broken meats* scraps **14** *three-suited* with three suits (the wardrobe allowed serving-men); *hundred-pound* (the minimal estate for anyone aspiring to gentility) **15** *worsted-stocking* (serving-men's attire) **15–16** *action-taking* i.e. cowardly (resorting to law instead of fighting) **16** *glass-gazing, superserviceable, finical* i.e. conceited, toadying, foppish **17** *inheriting* possessing **17–18** *a bawd . . . service* i.e. a pander, if pleasing your employer required it **19** *composition* composite **22** *addition* titles

71

Draw, you rogue, for though it be night, yet the moon
29   shines. I'll make a sop o' th' moonshine of you. You
30   whoreson cullionly barbermonger, draw!

OSWALD Away, I have nothing to do with thee.

KENT Draw, you rascal. You come with letters against the
33   King, and take Vanity the puppet's part against the
34   royalty of her father. Draw, you rogue, or I'll so car-
35   bonado your shanks. Draw, you rascal. Come your ways!

OSWALD Help, ho! Murder! Help!

37 KENT Strike, you slave! Stand, rogue! Stand, you neat
slave! Strike!
[Beats him.]

OSWALD Help, ho! Murder, murder!
Enter Bastard [Edmund, with his rapier drawn],
Cornwall, Regan, Gloucester, Servants.

EDMUND How now? What's the matter? Part!

41 KENT With you, goodman boy, if you please! Come, I'll
42   flesh ye; come on, young master.

GLOUCESTER Weapons? Arms? What's the matter here?

CORNWALL Keep peace, upon your lives. He dies that
strikes again. What is the matter?

REGAN The messengers from our sister and the King.

CORNWALL What is your difference? Speak.

OSWALD I am scarce in breath, my lord.

49 KENT No marvel, you have so bestirred your valor. You
50   cowardly rascal, Nature disclaims in thee. A tailor made
thee.

CORNWALL Thou art a strange fellow. A tailor make a
man?

---

29 *sop o' th' moonshine* i.e. something that sops up moonshine through its
perforations   30 *cullionly barbermonger* vile fop (i.e. always dealing with
hairdressers)   33 *Vanity the puppet* i.e. Goneril (here equated with a stock
figure in morality plays, now dwindled into puppet shows)   34 *carbonado*
(cut into strips or cubes)   35 *your ways* get along   37 *neat* primping   41
goodman boy (doubly contemptuous, since peasants were addressed as
'goodmen')   42 *flesh ye* give you your first taste of blood   49 *bestirred*
exercised   50 *disclaims* claims no part

KENT A tailor, sir. A stonecutter or a painter could not 53
have made him so ill, though they had been but two
years o' th' trade.

CORNWALL
Speak yet, how grew your quarrel?

OSWALD This ancient ruffian, sir, whose life I have
spared at suit of his gray beard –   58

KENT Thou whoreson zed, thou unnecessary letter! My 59
lord, if you will give me leave, I will tread this unbolted 60
villain into mortar and daub the wall of a jakes with him. 61
Spare my gray beard? you wagtail.   62

CORNWALL
Peace, sirrah!
You beastly knave, know you no reverence?   64

KENT
Yes, sir, but anger hath a privilege.

CORNWALL
Why art thou angry?

KENT
That such a slave as this should wear a sword,
Who wears no honesty. Such smiling rogues as these
Like rats oft bite the holy cords atwain   69
Which are too intrinse t' unloose; smooth every passion   70
That in the natures of their lords rebel,   71
Being oil to fire, snow to the colder moods;   72
Renege, affirm, and turn their halcyon beaks   73
With every gale and vary of their masters,   74

---

53 *stonecutter* sculptor 58 *at suit of* on the plea of, moved to mercy by
59 *zed* (last and least useful of letters) 60 *unbolted* unsifted, crude 61
jakes privy 62 *wagtail* (any of several birds whose tail-feathers wag or
bob, suggesting obsequiousness or effeminacy) 64 *beastly* beast-like,
irrational 69 *holy cords* sacred bonds (between parents and children,
husbands and wives, man and God) 70 *intrinse* intrinsic, inextricable;
smooth flatter, cater to 71 *rebel* (i.e. against reason and moral restraint)
72 *Being . . . moods* (i.e. feeders of intemperance) 73 *Renege* deny; *halcyon
beaks* kingfisher beaks (supposedly serving as weather vanes when the birds
were hung up by their necks) 74 *gale and vary* varying wind

Knowing naught, like dogs, but following.
76   A plague upon your epileptic visage!
77   Smile you my speeches, as I were a fool?
78   Goose, if I had you upon Sarum Plain,
79   I'ld drive ye cackling home to Camelot.

CORNWALL
What, art thou mad, old fellow?

GLOUCESTER
How fell you out? Say that.

KENT
82   No contraries hold more antipathy
Than I and such a knave.

CORNWALL
Why dost thou call him knave? What is his fault?

KENT
His countenance likes me not.

CORNWALL
No more perchance does mine, nor his, nor hers.

KENT
Sir, 'tis my occupation to be plain:
I have seen better faces in my time
Than stands on any shoulder that I see
Before me at this instant.

CORNWALL   This is some fellow
Who, having been praised for bluntness, doth affect
92   A saucy roughness, and constrains the garb
Quite from his nature. He cannot flatter, he;
An honest mind and plain – he must speak truth.
An they will take it, so; if not, he's plain.
These kind of knaves I know which in this plainness
Harbor more craft and more corrupter ends

---

76 *epileptic* contorted in a grin (?)   77 *Smile you* smile you at, mock you
78 *Sarum Plain* Salisbury Plain (said to have been associated with geese,
but the allusion remains cryptic)   79 *Camelot* legendary seat of King
Arthur, variously sited at Winchester, near Cadbury, in Wales, etc.
82 *contraries* opposites   92–93 *constrains . . . nature* distorts the plain
fashion from its true nature, caricatures it

Than twenty silly-ducking observants   98
That stretch their duties nicely.   99

KENT
Sir, in good faith, in sincere verity,
Under th' allowance of your great aspect,   101
Whose influence, like the wreath of radiant fire   102
On flick'ring Phoebus' front —   103

CORNWALL   What mean'st by this?

KENT To go out of my dialect, which you discommend so   104
much. I know, sir, I am no flatterer. He that beguiled   105
you in a plain accent was a plain knave, which, for my
part, I will not be, though I should win your displeasure   107
to entreat me to't.

CORNWALL
What was th' offense you gave him?

OSWALD
I never gave him any.
It pleased the King his master very late   111
To strike at me, upon his misconstruction;   112
When he, compact, and flattering his displeasure,   113
Tripped me behind; being down, insulted, railed,
And put upon him such a deal of man   115
That worthied him, got praises of the King   116
For him attempting who was self-subdued;   117
And, in the fleshment of this dread exploit,   118
Drew on me here again.

---

98 *silly-ducking observants* ludicrously bowing form-servers **99** *nicely*
fussily **101** *allowance* approval; *aspect* (1) appearance, (2) heavenly
position **102** *influence* astrological force **103** *Phoebus' front* sun's fore-
head (i.e. face) **104** *go . . . dialect* depart from my way of speaking **105**
He (the type of plain-speaker Cornwall has condemned) **107–08** *though
. . . to't* though I should persuade your disapproving self to beg me to do so
(? with *displeasure* sarcastically substituted for 'grace') **111** *very late*
quite recently **112** *misconstruction* misunderstanding **113** *compact* in
league with **115** *And put . . . man* i.e. affected such excessive manliness
116 *worthied* enhanced his worth **117** *For him . . . self-subdued* for assail-
ing him (Oswald) who chose not to resist **118** *fleshment of* bloodthirsti-
ness induced by

119 KENT   None of these rogues and cowards
But Ajax is their fool.

CORNWALL   Fetch forth the stocks!
121   You stubborn ancient knave, you reverent braggart,
We'll teach you.

KENT   Sir, I am too old to learn.
Call not your stocks for me, I serve the King—
On whose employment I was sent to you;
125   You shall do small respect, show too bold malice
126   Against the grace and person of my master,
Stocking his messenger.

CORNWALL
Fetch forth the stocks. As I have life and honor,
There shall he sit till noon.

REGAN
Till noon? Till night, my lord, and all night too.

KENT
Why, madam, if I were your father's dog,
You should not use me so.

REGAN   Sir, being his knave, I will.

CORNWALL
133   This is a fellow of the selfsame color
134   Our sister speaks of. Come, bring away the stocks.
Stocks brought out.

GLOUCESTER
Let me beseech your Grace not to do so.
[His fault is much, and the good King his master
137   Will check him for't. Your purposed low correction
138   Is such as basest and contemnèd'st wretches
For pilf'rings and most common trespasses
Are punished with.]

119–20 *None . . . fool* i.e. the Ajax type, stupidly belligerent, is the favorite
butt of cowardly rogues like Oswald   121 *stubborn* rude; *reverent* aged
125 *malice* ill will   126 *grace* royal honor   133 *color* kind   134 *away* along
137 *check* rebuke; *purposed* intended   138 *contemnèd'st* most harshly
sentenced

The King his master needs must take it ill
That he, so slightly valued in his messenger,   142
Should have him thus restrained.

CORNWALL   I'll answer that.   143

REGAN
My sister may receive it much more worse,
To have her gentleman abused, assaulted,
[For following her affairs. Put in his legs.]
    [Kent is put in the stocks.]

CORNWALL
Come, my lord, away!
                    Exit [with all but Gloucester and Kent].

GLOUCESTER
I am sorry for thee, friend. 'Tis the Duke's pleasure,
Whose disposition all the world well knows   149
Will not be rubbed nor stopped. I'll entreat for thee.   150

KENT
Pray do not, sir. I have watched and travelled hard.   151
Some time I shall sleep out, the rest I'll whistle.
A good man's fortune may grow out at heels.   153
Give you good morrow.   154

GLOUCESTER
The Duke's to blame in this. 'Twill be ill taken.   *Exit.*   155

KENT
Good King, that must approve the common saw,   156
Thou out of heaven's benediction com'st   157
To the warm sun.
Approach, thou beacon to this under globe,   159
That by thy comfortable beams I may

---

142 *slightly valued in* i.e. little respected in the person of 143 *answer*
answer for 149 *disposition* inclination 150 *rubbed* deflected (bowling
term) 151 *watched* gone sleepless 153 *A good . . . heels* i.e. it is no
disgrace to decline in fortune 154 *Give* God give 155 *taken* received
156 *approve* demonstrate the truth of; *saw* saying, proverb 157–58
Thou . . . sun (proverb, meaning from better to worse, i.e. from heavenly
shelter to earthly exposure – 'the heat of the day') 159 *beacon . . . globe*
i.e. the sun (here viewed as benign)

161　Peruse this letter. Nothing almost sees miracles
　　　But misery. I know 'tis from Cordelia,
　　　Who hath most fortunately been informed
164　Of my obscurèd course. And shall find time
165　From this enormous state, seeking to give
166　Losses their remedies. – All weary and o'erwatched,
167　Take vantage, heavy eyes, not to behold
168　This shameful lodging. Fortune, good night;
169　Smile once more; turn thy wheel.
　　　　　[Sleeps.]

II, iii　　　　*Enter Edgar.*

EDGAR
　　　I heard myself proclaimed,
2　　And by the happy hollow of a tree
　　　Escaped the hunt. No port is free, no place
　　　That guard and most unusual vigilance
5　　Does not attend my taking. Whiles I may 'scape,
6　　I will preserve myself; and am bethought
　　　To take the basest and most poorest shape
　　　That ever penury, in contempt of man,
　　　Brought near to beast: my face I'll grime with filth,
10　Blanket my loins, elf all my hairs in knots,
11　And with presented nakedness outface
　　　The winds and persecutions of the sky.
13　The country gives me proof and precedent
14　Of Bedlam beggars, who, with roaring voices,
15　Strike in their numbed and mortified bare arms
16　Pins, wooden pricks, nails, sprigs of rosemary;

161–62 *Nothing . . . misery* i.e. miraculous aid is seldom seen (or searched for?) except by the miserable　164 *obscurèd* disguised　164–66 *And . . . remedies* (incoherent: perhaps corrupt, or perhaps snatches read from the letter)　165 *enormous state* monstrous situation　166 *Losses* reverses　167 *vantage* i.e. advantage of sleep　168 *lodging* (in the stocks)　169 *wheel* (Fortune's wheel was represented as vertical. Kent is at its bottom.)
II, iii　2 *happy hollow* i.e. lucky hiding-place　5 *attend my taking* contemplate my capture　6 *bethought* in mind　10 *elf* tangle (into 'elf-locks')　11 *presented* a show of　13 *proof* example　14 *Bedlam* (see I, ii, 131–32n.)　15 *Strike* stick; *mortified* deadened to pain　16 *pricks* skewers

And with this horrible object, from low farms,   17
Poor pelting villages, sheepcotes, and mills,   18
Sometimes with lunatic bans, sometime with prayers,   19
Enforce their charity. Poor Turlygod, poor Tom,   20
That's something yet : Edgar I nothing am.   21

                                              Exit.

Enter Lear, Fool, and Gentleman.   II, iv

LEAR
'Tis strange that they should so depart from home,
And not send back my messenger.

GENTLEMAN   As I learned,
The night before there was no purpose in them   3
Of this remove.   4

KENT   Hail to thee, noble master.

LEAR Ha !
Mak'st thou this shame thy pastime ?

KENT   No, my lord.

FOOL Ha, ha, he wears cruel garters. Horses are tied by   7
the heads, dogs and bears by th' neck, monkeys by th'
loins, and men by th' legs. When a man 's over-lusty at   9
legs, then he wears wooden nether-stocks.   10

LEAR
What's he that hath so much thy place mistook
To set thee here ?

KENT   It is both he and she,
Your son and daughter.

LEAR No.

KENT Yes.

LEAR No, I say.

KENT I say yea.

[LEAR No, no, they would not.

---

17 *object* picture 18 *pelting* paltry 19 *bans* curses 20 *Turlygod* (un-
identified, but evidently another name for a Tom o' Bedlam) 21 *Edgar* i.e.
as Edgar
II, iv 3 *purpose* intention 4 *remove* removal 7 *cruel* painful (with pun
on 'crewel,' a yarn used in garters) 9–10 *over-lusty at legs* i.e. too much on
the go (?), or too much given to kicking (?) 10 *nether-stocks* stockings (as
distinct from 'upper-stocks' or breeches)

KENT Yes, they have.]

LEAR
By Jupiter, I swear no!

KENT
By Juno, I swear ay!

LEAR   They durst not do't;
They could not, would not do't. 'Tis worse than murder
23   To do upon respect such violent outrage.
24   Resolve me with all modest haste which way
Thou mightst deserve or thy impose this usage,
Coming from us.

KENT   My lord, when at their home
27   I did commend your Highness' letters to them,
Ere I was risen from the place that showed
My duty kneeling, came there a reeking post,
30   Stewed in his haste, half breathless, panting forth
From Goneril his mistress salutations;
32   Delivered letters, spite of intermission,
33   Which presently they read; on whose contents
34   They summoned up their meiny, straight took horse,
Commanded me to follow and attend
The leisure of their answer, gave me cold looks;
And meeting here the other messenger,
Whose welcome I perceived had poisoned mine,
Being the very fellow which of late
40   Displayed so saucily against your Highness,
41   Having more man than wit about me, drew;
42   He raised the house with loud and coward cries.
Your son and daughter found this trespass worth
The shame which here it suffers.

45 FOOL Winter's not gone yet, if the wild geese fly that way.

---

23 *To . . . outrage* i.e. to show such outrageous disrespect **24** *Resolve* enlighten; *modest* seemly **27** *commend* entrust **30** *Stewed* steaming **32** *spite of intermission* in disregard of its being an interruption **33** *presently* immediately; *on* on the strength of **34** *meiny* attendants **40** *Displayed* showed off **41** *man* manhood; *wit* sense **42** *raised* aroused **45** *Winter's . . . way* i.e. the ill season continues according to these signs (with Cornwall and Regan equated with *wild geese*, proverbially evasive)

Fathers that wear rags
  Do make their children blind,   47
But fathers that bear bags   48
  Shall see their children kind.
Fortune, that arrant whore,   50
Ne'er turns the key to th' poor.   51
But for all this, thou shalt have as many dolors for thy 52
daughters as thou canst tell in a year.   53

LEAR
O, how this mother swells up toward my heart!   54
Hysterica passio, down, thou climbing sorrow;   55
Thy element's below. Where is this daughter?   56

KENT
With the Earl, sir, here within.

LEAR   Follow me not;
Stay here.   *Exit.*

GENTLEMAN
Made you no more offense but what you speak of?

KENT None.
How chance the King comes with so small a number?

FOOL An thou hadst been set i' th' stocks for that question, thou'dst well deserved it.

KENT Why, fool?

FOOL We'll set thee to school to an ant, to teach thee
there's no laboring i' th' winter. All that follow their 66
noses are led by their eyes but blind men, and there's not
a nose among twenty but can smell him that's stinking.
Let go thy hold when a great wheel runs down a hill, lest
it break thy neck with following. But the great one that
goes upward, let him draw thee after. When a wise man

47 *blind* (to their fathers' needs)   48 *bags* (of gold)   50 *Fortune . . . whore*
(because so fickle and callous)   51 *turns the key* i.e. opens the door   52
dolors sorrows (with pun on 'dollars,' continental coins)   53 *tell* count
54, 55 *mother, Hysterica passio* hysteria (the popular and the medical
terms)   56 *element* proper place   66 *no laboring . . . winter* (Lear, accompanied by *so small a number*, is equated with winter bereft of workers, such
as ants)   66–68 *All . . . stinking* i.e. almost anyone can smell out a person
decayed in fortune

gives thee better counsel, give me mine again. I would
73 have none but knaves follow it since a fool gives it.

       That sir which serves and seeks for gain,
75   And follows but for form,
76   Will pack when it begins to rain
           And leave thee in the storm.
       But I will tarry; the fool will stay,
           And let the wise man fly.
80   The knave turns fool that runs away;
81   The fool no knave, perdy.

KENT Where learned you this, fool?
83 FOOL Not i' th' stocks, fool.
       Enter Lear and Gloucester.

LEAR
   Deny to speak with me? They are sick, they are weary,
85 They have travelled all the night? Mere fetches,
86 The images of revolt and flying off!
   Fetch me a better answer.
GLOUCESTER   My dear lord,
88 You know the fiery quality of the Duke,
   How unremovable and fixed he is
   In his own course.
LEAR   Vengeance, plague, death, confusion!
   Fiery? What quality? Why, Gloucester, Gloucester,
   I'ld speak with the Duke of Cornwall and his wife.
GLOUCESTER
   Well, my good lord, I have informed them so.
LEAR
   Informed them? Dost thou understand me, man?
GLOUCESTER
   Ay, my good lord.

---

73 *none but knaves* (here and in what follows the Fool repudiates his advice
to abandon Lear) **75** *form* show **76** *pack* be off **80** *The knave . . . away*
i.e. faithlessness is the true folly **81** *perdy* I swear (from '*par dieu*') **83**
fool (persiflage, but also a term of honour; cf. V, iii, 306n.) **85** *fetches*
counterfeit reasons, false likenesses of truth **86** *images* true likenesses;
flying off revolt **88** *quality* disposition

LEAR

The King would speak with Cornwall. The dear father
Would with his daughter speak, commands – tends –   97
    service.
Are they informed of this ? My breath and blood !
Fiery ? The fiery Duke, tell the hot Duke that –
No, but not yet. May be he is not well.
Infirmity doth still neglect all office   101
Whereto our health is bound. We are not ourselves   102
When nature, being oppressed, commands the mind
To suffer with the body. I'll forbear ;
And am fallen out with my more headier will   105
To take the indisposed and sickly fit
For the sound man. – Death on my state ! Wherefore
Should he sit here ? This act persuades me   108
That this remotion of the Duke and her   109
Is practice only. Give me my servant forth.   110
Go tell the Duke and 's wife I'ld speak with them !
Now, presently ! Bid them come forth and hear me,   112
Or at their chamber door I'll beat the drum
Till it cry sleep to death.   114

GLOUCESTER

I would have all well betwixt you.   *Exit.*

LEAR

O me, my heart, my rising heart ! But down !

FOOL Cry to it, nuncle, as the cockney did to the eels when 117
she put 'em i' th' paste alive. She knapped 'em o' th' cox-   118
combs with a stick and cried, 'Down, wantons, down !'   119
'Twas her brother that, in pure kindness to his horse,
buttered his hay.   121

---

97 *tends* attends, awaits (?), tenders, offers (?)   **101** *all office* duties   **102** *Whereto . . . bound* to which, in health, we are bound   **105** *headier* head-strong   **108** *he* i.e. Kent   **109** *remotion* remaining remote, inaccessible   **110** *practice* trickery   **112** *presently* immediately   **114** *cry* pursue with noise (like a pack or 'cry' of hounds)   **117** *cockney* city-dweller   **118** *paste* pastry pie; *knapped* rapped   **119** *wantons* i.e. frisky things   **121** *buttered his hay* (another example of rustic humor at the expense of cockney inexperience)

Enter Cornwall, Regan, Gloucester, Servants.

LEAR
Good morrow to you both.

CORNWALL   Hail to your Grace.

Kent here set at liberty.

REGAN
I am glad to see your Highness.

LEAR
Regan, I think you are. I know what reason
I have to think so. If thou shouldst not be glad,
126 I would divorce me from thy mother's tomb,
Sepulchring an adultress. *[to Kent]* O, are you free?
Some other time for that. – Beloved Regan,
Thy sister's naught. O Regan, she hath tied
Sharp-toothed unkindness, like a vulture, here.
I can scarce speak to thee. Thou'lt not believe
132 With how depraved a quality – O Regan!

REGAN
133 I pray you, sir, take patience. I have hope
You less know how to value her desert
135 Than she to scant her duty.

LEAR   Say? How is that?

REGAN
I cannot think my sister in the least
Would fail her obligation. If, sir, perchance
She have restrained the riots of your followers,
'Tis on such ground, and to such wholesome end,
As clears her from all blame.

LEAR
My curses on her!

REGAN   O, sir, you are old;
142 Nature in you stands on the very verge

126–27 *divorce . . . adultress* i.e. refuse to be buried with your mother
since such a child as you must have been conceived in adultery   132 *how
. . . quality* i.e. what innate depravity   133 *have hope* i.e. suspect   135
scant (in effect, a double negative; 'do' would be more logical though less
emphatic)   142–43 *Nature . . . confine* i.e. your life nears the limit of its
tenure

Of his confine. You should be ruled, and led
By some discretion that discerns your state   144
Better than you yourself. Therefore I pray you
That to our sister you do make return;
Say you have wronged her.

LEAR   Ask her forgiveness?
Do you but mark how this becomes the house: 148
'Dear daughter, I confess that I am old.
          [Kneels.]
Age is unnecessary. On my knees I beg
That you'll vouchsafe me raiment, bed, and food.'

REGAN
Good sir, no more. These are unsightly tricks.
Return you to my sister.

LEAR [rises]   Never, Regan.
She hath abated me of half my train,   154
Looked black upon me, struck me with her tongue
Most serpent-like upon the very heart.
All the stored vengeances of heaven fall
On her ingrateful top! Strike her young bones,   158
You taking airs, with lameness.   159

CORNWALL   Fie, sir, fie!

LEAR
You nimble lightnings, dart your blinding flames
Into her scornful eyes! Infect her beauty,
You fen-sucked fogs drawn by the pow'rful sun   162
To fall and blister –   163

REGAN   O the blessed gods!
So will you wish on me when the rash mood is on.

LEAR
No, Regan, thou shalt never have my curse.
Thy tender-hefted nature shall not give   166

144 *some discretion . . . state* someone discerning enough to recognize your
condition   148 *the house* household or family decorum   154 *abated*
curtailed   158 *ingrateful top* ungrateful head   159 *taking* infectious
162 *fen-sucked* drawn up from swamps   163 *fall and blister* strike and raise
blisters (such as those of smallpox)   166 *tender-hefted* swayed by tender-
ness, gently disposed

Thee o'er to harshness. Her eyes are fierce, but thine
Do comfort, and not burn. 'Tis not in thee
To grudge my pleasures, to cut off my train,
170   To bandy hasty words, to scant my sizes,
171   And, in conclusion, to oppose the bolt
Against my coming in. Thou better know'st
173   The offices of nature, bond of childhood,
174   Effects of courtesy, dues of gratitude.
Thy half o' th' kingdom hast thou not forgot,
Wherein I thee endowed.
176 REGAN   Good sir, to th' purpose.
          Tucket within.

LEAR
Who put my man i' th' stocks?
CORNWALL   What trumpet's that?
REGAN
178   I know't—my sister's. This approves her letter,
That she would soon be here.
          Enter Steward [Oswald]. Is your lady come?

LEAR
180   This is a slave, whose easy-borrowèd pride
181   Dwells in the fickle grace of her he follows.
182   Out, varlet, from my sight.
CORNWALL   What means your Grace?
LEAR
Who stocked my servant? Regan, I have good hope
Thou didst not know on't.
          Enter Goneril.   Who comes here? O heavens!
If you do love old men, if your sweet sway
186   Allow obedience, if you yourselves are old,
187   Make it your cause. Send down, and take my part.

---

170 *bandy* volley; *sizes* allowances   **171** *oppose the bolt* i.e. bar the door
173 *offices of nature* natural duties   **174** *Effects* actions   **176** *purpose* point
178 *approves* confirms   **180** *easy-borrowèd* acquired on small security   **181**
grace favor   **182** *varlet* low fellow   **186** *Allow* approve   **187** *Make . . . cause*
i.e. make my cause yours

[To Goneril]
Art not ashamed to look upon this beard?
O Regan, will you take her by the hand?

GONERIL
Why not by th' hand, sir? How have I offended?
All's not offense that indiscretion finds   191
And dotage terms so.

LEAR   O sides, you are too tough!   192
Will you yet hold? How came my man i' th' stocks?

CORNWALL
I set him there, sir; but his own disorders
Deserved much less advancement.   195

LEAR   You? Did you?

REGAN
I pray you, father, being weak, seem so.   196
If till the expiration of your month
You will return and sojourn with my sister,
Dismissing half your train, come then to me.
I am now from home, and out of that provision
Which shall be needful for your entertainment.   201

LEAR
Return to her, and fifty men dismissed?
No, rather I abjure all roofs, and choose
To wage against the emnity o' th' air,   204
To be a comrade with the wolf and owl,
Necessity's sharp pinch. Return with her?   206
Why, the hot-blooded France, that dowerless took   207
Our youngest born, I could as well be brought
To knee his throne, and, squire-like, pension beg 209
To keep base life afoot. Return with her?

---

191 *indiscretion finds* ill judgment detects as such   **192** *sides* breast (which should burst with grief)   **195** *less advancement* i.e. more abasement   **196** *seem so* i.e. act the part   **201** *entertainment* lodging   **204** *wage* fight   **206** *Necessity's sharp pinch* (a summing up of the hardships previously listed)   **207** *hot-blooded* choleric (cf. I, ii, 23)   **209** *knee* kneel at; *squire-like* like an attendant

211   Persuade me rather to be slave and sumpter
212   To this detested groom.

GONERIL   At your choice, sir.

LEAR
       I prithee, daughter, do not make me mad.
       I will not trouble thee, my child ; farewell.
       We'll no more meet, no more see one another.
       But yet thou art my flesh, my blood, my daughter ;
       Or rather a disease that's in my flesh,
       Which I must needs call mine. Thou art a boil,
219   A plague-sore, or embossèd carbuncle
       In my corrupted blood. But I'll not chide thee.
       Let shame come when it will, I do not call it.
222   I do not bid the thunder-bearer shoot,
223   Nor tell tales of thee to high-judging Jove.
       Mend when thou canst, be better at thy leisure ;
       I can be patient, I can stay with Regan,
       I and my hundred knights.

REGAN   Not altogether so.
       I looked not for you yet, nor am provided
       For your fit welcome. Give ear, sir, to my sister ;
229   For those that mingle reason with your passion
       Must be content to think you old and so –
       But she knows what she does.

LEAR   Is this well spoken ?

REGAN
232   I dare avouch it, sir. What, fifty followers ?
       Is it not well ? What should you need of more ?
234   Yea, or so many, sith that both charge and danger
       Speak 'gainst so great a number ? How in one house
       Should many people, under two commands,
       Hold amity ? 'Tis hard, almost impossible.

---

211 *sumpter* packhorse 212 *groom* i.e. Oswald 219 *embossèd* risen to a
head 222 *thunder-bearer* i.e. Jupiter 223 *high-judging* judging from on
high 229 *mingle : . . passion* interpret your passion in the light of reason
232 *avouch* swear by 234 *sith that* since ; *charge* expense

GONERIL
    Why might not you, my lord, receive attendance
    From those that she calls servants, or from mine?

REGAN
    Why not, my lord? If then they chanced to slack ye,   240
    We could control them. If you will come to me
    (For now I spy a danger), I entreat you
    To bring but five-and-twenty. To no more
    Will I give place or notice.   244

LEAR
    I gave you all.

REGAN   And in good time you gave it.

LEAR
    Made you my guardians, my depositaries,   246
    But kept a reservation to be followèd   247
    With such a number. What, must I come to you
    With five-and-twenty? Regan, said you so?

REGAN
    And speak't again, my lord. No more with me.

LEAR
    Those wicked creatures yet do look well-favored   251
    When others are more wicked; not being the worst
    Stands in some rank of praise.   253
        [To Goneril]   I'll go with thee.
    Thy fifty yet doth double five-and-twenty,
    And thou art twice her love.   255

GONERIL   Hear me, my lord.
    What need you five-and-twenty? ten? or five?
    To follow in a house where twice so many
    Have a command to tend you?

REGAN   What need one?

---

240 *slack* neglect 244 *notice* recognition 246 *depositaries* trustees
247 *kept . . . to be* stipulated that I be 251 *well-favored* comely 253
Stands . . . praise i.e. is at least relatively praiseworthy 255 *her love* i.e. as
loving as she

Test?

LEAR

259 O reason not the need ! Our basest beggars
260 Are in the poorest thing superfluous.
261 Allow not nature more than nature needs,
     Man's life is cheap as beast's. Thou art a lady :
263 If only to go warm were gorgeous,
     Why, nature needs not what thou gorgeous wear'st,
     Which scarcely keeps thee warm. But, for true need –
     You heavens, give me that patience, patience I need.
     You see me here, you gods, a poor old man,
     As full of grief as age, wretched in both.
     If it be you that stirs these daughters' hearts
270 Against their father, fool me not so much
     To bear it tamely ; touch me with noble anger,
     And let not women's weapons, water drops,
     Stain my man's cheeks. No, you unnatural hags !
     I will have such revenges on you both
     That all the world shall – I will do such things –
     What they are, yet I know not ; but they shall be
     The terrors of the earth. You think I'll weep.
     No, I'll not weep.
          Storm and tempest.
     I have full cause of weeping, but this heart
280 Shall break into a hundred thousand flaws
281 Or ere I'll weep. O fool, I shall go mad !
          Exeunt [Lear, Fool, Kent, and Gloucester].

CORNWALL
     Let us withdraw ; 'twill be a storm.

REGAN
     This house is little ; the old man and 's people
     Cannot be well bestowed.

---

259 *reason* analyze   **260** *Are . . . superfluous* i.e. have some poor possession
not utterly indispensable   **261** *than nature needs* i.e. than life needs for
mere survival   **263–65** *If . . . warm* i.e. if to be dressed warmly (i.e. for
need) were considered sufficiently gorgeous, you would not need your
present attire, which is gorgeous rather than warm   **270** *fool* play with,
humiliate   **280** *flaws* fragments   **281** *Or ere* before

GONERIL
  'Tis his own blame ; hath put himself from rest   285
  And must needs taste his folly.

REGAN
  For his particular, I'll receive him gladly,   287
  But not one follower.

GONERIL   So am I purposed.   288
  Where is my Lord of Gloucester ?

CORNWALL
  Followèd the old man forth.
     [Enter Gloucester.]   He is returned.

GLOUCESTER
  The King is in high rage.

CORNWALL   Whither is he going ?

GLOUCESTER
  He calls to horse, but will I know not whither.

CORNWALL
  'Tis best to give him way ; he leads himself.

GONERIL
  My lord, entreat him by no means to stay.

GLOUCESTER
  Alack, the night comes on, and the high winds
  Do sorely ruffle. For many miles about   296
  There's scarce a bush.

REGAN   O, sir, to willful men
  The injuries that they themselves procure
  Must be their schoolmasters. Shut up your doors.
  He is attended with a desperate train,
  And what they may incense him to, being apt   301
  To have his ear abused, wisdom bids fear.

CORNWALL
  Shut up your doors, my lord ; 'tis a wild night.
  My Regan counsels well. Come out o' th' storm.   *Exeunt.*

*

285 *hath . . . rest* i.e. is responsible for leaving his resting place with her (?),
is self-afflicted (?) 287 *particular* own person 288 *purposed* determined
296 *ruffle* rage 301–02 *apt . . . abused* i.e. predisposed to listen to ill counsel

III, i   *Storm still. Enter Kent and a Gentleman severally.*

KENT
Who's there besides foul weather?

GENTLEMAN
2   One minded like the weather, most unquietly.

KENT
I know you. Where's the King?

GENTLEMAN
4   Contending with the fretful elements;
Bids the wind blow the earth into the sea,
6   Or swell the curlèd waters 'bove the main,
7   That things might change or cease; [tears his white hair,
8   Which the impetuous blasts, with eyeless rage,
Catch in their fury and make nothing of;
10 Strives in his little world of man to outscorn
The to-and-fro-conflicting wind and rain.
12 This night, wherein the cub-drawn bear would couch,
13 The lion and the belly-pinchèd wolf
Keep their fur dry, unbonneted he runs,
15 And bids what will take all.]
KENT   But who is with him?

GENTLEMAN
None but the fool, who labors to outjest
His heart-struck injuries.
KENT   Sir, I do know you,
18 And dare upon the warrant of my note
19 Commend a dear thing to you. There is division,
Although as yet the face of it is covered
With mutual cunning, 'twixt Albany and Cornwall;
22 Who have – as who have not, that their great stars

III, i An open heath   **2** *minded . . . unquietly* i.e. in disturbed mood   **4**
Contending quarrelling   **6** *main* mainland   **7** *change* revert to chaos (?),
improve (?)   **8** *eyeless* (1) blind, (2) invisible   **10** *little world* (the 'microcosm,' which is disturbed like the great world or 'macrocosm')   **12** *cub-
drawn* cub-sucked (and hence ravenous)   **13** *belly-pinchèd* famished
15 *take all* (the cry of the desperate gambler in staking his last)   **18** *warrant
. . . note* assurance of my knowledge   **19** *Commend . . . thing* entrust a
precious matter   **22** *that* whom; *stars* destinies

Throned and set high? – servants, who seem no less,   23
Which are to France the spies and speculations   24
Intelligent of our state. What hath been seen,   25
Either in snuffs and packings of the Dukes,   26
Or the hard rein which both of them have borne   27
Against the old kind King, or something deeper,
Whereof, perchance, these are but furnishings –   29
[But, true it is, from France there comes a power   30
Into this scatterèd kingdom, who already,   31
Wise in our negligence, have secret feet
In some of our best ports and are at point
To show their open banner. Now to you:
If on my credit you dare build so far   35
To make your speed to Dover, you shall find
Some that will thank you, making just report
Of how unnatural and bemadding sorrow   38
The King hath cause to plain.   39
I am a gentleman of blood and breeding,
And from some knowledge and assurance offer
This office to you.]   42

GENTLEMAN
    I will talk further with you.

KENT   No, do not.
For confirmation that I am much more
Than my out-wall, open this purse and take   45
What it contains. If you shall see Cordelia,
As fear not but you shall, show her this ring,
And she will tell you who that fellow is
That yet you do not know. Fie on this storm!
I will go seek the King.

GENTLEMAN
    Give me your hand. Have you no more to say?

---

23 *Throned* have throned; *no less* i.e. truly so   24 *speculations* spies   25
Intelligent supplying intelligence   26 *snuffs* quarrels; *packings* intrigues
27 *hard rein . . . borne* i.e. harsh curbs . . . exercised   29 *furnishings* pretexts
30 *power* army   31 *scatterèd* divided   35 *my credit* trust in me; *build* take
constructive action   38 *bemadding sorrow* maddening grievances   39 *plain*
lament   42 *office* service   45 *out-wall* surface appearance

KENT

52   Few words, but, to effect, more than all yet:
53   That when we have found the King – in which your pain
     That way, I'll this – he that first lights on him
     Holla the other.   *Exeunt [severally]*.

*

III, ii   *Storm still. Enter Lear and Fool.*

LEAR

Blow, winds, and crack your cheeks. Rage, blow.
2   You cataracts and hurricanoes, spout
3   Till you have drenched our steeples, drowned the cocks.
4   You sulph'rous and thought-executing fires,
5   Vaunt-couriers of oak-cleaving thunderbolts,
     Singe my white head. And thou, all-shaking thunder,
     Strike flat the thick rotundity o' th' world,
8   Crack Nature's moulds, all germains spill at once,
     That makes ingrateful man.

10   FOOL O nuncle, court holy-water in a dry house is better
     than this rain-water out o' door. Good nuncle, in; ask
     thy daughters blessing. Here's a night pities neither
     wise men nor fools.

LEAR

Rumble thy bellyful. Spit, fire. Spout, rain.
Nor rain, wind, thunder, fire are my daughters.
16   I tax not you, you elements, with unkindness.
     I never gave you kingdom, called you children;
18   You owe me no subscription. Then let fall
19   Your horrible pleasure. Here I stand your slave,
     A poor, infirm, weak, and despised old man.

---

52 *to effect* in their import   **53** *pain* pains, care
III, ii The same   **2** *hurricanoes* water-spouts   **3** *cocks* weathercocks
4 *thought-executing fires* i.e. flashes of lightning swift as thought (?),
dazing, benumbing the mind (?)   **5** *Vaunt-couriers* heralds   **8** *moulds* (in
which Nature's creations are formed); *germains* seeds   **10** *court holy-water*
flattery (slang)   **16** *tax* charge   **18** *subscription* deference   **19** *pleasure*
will

But yet I call you servile ministers,   21
That will with two pernicious daughters join
Your high-engendered battles 'gainst a head   23
So old and white as this. O, ho ! 'tis foul.

FOOL He that has a house to put 's head in has a good
    headpiece.

        The codpiece that will house   27
          Before the head has any,
        The head and he shall louse :   29
          So beggars marry many.   30
        The man that makes his toe   31
          What he his heart should make
        Shall of a corn cry woe,
          And turn his sleep to wake.

For there was never yet fair woman but she made   35
    mouths in a glass.
        Enter Kent.

LEAR
    No, I will be the pattern of all patience ;
    I will say nothing.

KENT Who's there ?

FOOL Marry, here's grace and a codpiece ; that's a wise
    man and a fool.

KENT
    Alas, sir, are you here ? Things that love night
    Love not such nights as these. The wrathful skies
    Gallow the very wanderers of the dark   44
    And make them keep their caves. Since I was man,   45

---

21 *ministers* agents   **23** *high-engendered battles* heavenly battalions   **27–30**
The codpiece . . . many (the moral of the rime is that improvident cohabita-
tion spells penury)   **27** *codpiece* padded gusset at the crotch of the breeches
(slang for penis)   **29** *he* it   **30** *many* (head-lice and body-lice, accompany-
ing poverty)   **31–34** *The man . . . wake* (a parallel instance of misery
deriving from reckless impulse: to transpose the tender and precious
heart and the tough and base toe is to invite injury; with *heart* also suggesting Cordelia)   **35–36** *made . . . glass* i.e. posed before a mirror (irrelevant, except as vanity is a form of folly, the Fool's general theme)   **44**
Gallow frighten   **45** *keep their caves* i.e. keep under cover

46 Such sheets of fire, such bursts of horrid thunder,
   Such groans of roaring wind and rain, I never
48 Remember to have heard. Man's nature cannot carry
   Th' affliction nor the fear.

LEAR   Let the great gods
50 That keep this dreadful pudder o'er our heads
51 Find out their enemies now. Tremble, thou wretch,
   That hast within thee undivulgèd crimes
   Unwhipped of justice. Hide thee, thou bloody hand,
54 Thou perjured, and thou simular of virtue
   That art incestuous. Caitiff, to pieces shake,
56 That under covert and convenient seeming
57 Has practiced on man's life. Close pent-up guilts,
58 Rive your concealing continents and cry
59 These dreadful summoners grace. I am a man
   More sinned against than sinning.

KENT   Alack, bareheaded?
61 Gracious my lord, hard by here is a hovel;
   Some friendship will it lend you 'gainst the tempest.
63 Repose you there, while I to this hard house
   (More harder than the stones whereof 'tis raised,
65 Which even but now, demanding after you,
   Denied me to come in) return, and force
67 Their scanted courtesy.

LEAR   My wits begin to turn.
   Come on, my boy. How dost, my boy? Art cold?
   I am cold myself. Where is this straw, my fellow?
70 The art of our necessities is strange,
   And can make vile things precious. Come, your hovel.
   Poor fool and knave, I have one part in my heart

---

46 *horrid* horrible   48 *carry* bear   50 *pudder* turmoil   51 *Find . . . enemies*
i.e. discover sinners (by their show of fear)   54 *simular* counterfeit   56
seeming hypocrisy   57 *practiced on* plotted against; *Close* secret   58 *Rive*
split, break through; *continents* containers, covers   59 *summoners* arresting
officers of ecclesiastical courts; *grace* mercy   61 *Gracious my lord* my
gracious lord   63 *house* household (both building and occupants)   65
demanding after inquiring for   67 *scanted* stinted   70 *art* magic skill (as in
alchemy)

That's sorry yet for thee.

FOOL [sings]
> He that has and a little tiny wit,
>> With, heigh-ho, the wind and the rain,
> Must make content with his fortunes fit   76
>> Though the rain it raineth every day.

LEAR True, boy. Come, bring us to this hovel.

Exit [with Kent].

FOOL This is a brave night to cool a courtesan. I'll speak a   79
prophecy ere I go:
> When priests are more in word than matter;   81
> When brewers mar their malt with water;   82
> When nobles are their tailors' tutors,   83
> No heretics burned, but wenches' suitors;   84
> When every case in law is right,
> No squire in debt nor no poor knight;
> When slanders do not live in tongues,
> Nor cutpurses come not to throngs;
> When usurers tell their gold i' th' field,   89
> And bawds and whores do churches build –
> Then shall the realm of Albion   91
> Come to great confusion.   92
> Then comes the time, who lives to see't,
> That going shall be used with feet.   94
This prophecy Merlin shall make, for I live before his   95
time.   *Exit.*

*

76 *make . . . fit* i.e. reconcile himself to his fortunes   79 *brave* fine   81
are . . . matter i.e. can outshine the gospel message (At present their ability
to speak is quite unworthy of their theme.)   82 *mar* i.e. dilute (At present
they dilute water with malt, producing very small beer.)   83 *are . . . tutors*
i.e. are no longer subservient to fashion (Each subsequent line also reverses
the present state of affairs.)   84 *burned* (pun on contracting venereal
disease); *wenches' suitors* i.e. libertines   89 *tell* count; *i' th' field* (instead
of in secret places)   91 *Albion* England   92 *confusion* ruin (ironic: an
edifice of abuses is 'ruined' by reform)   94 *going . . . feet* walking will
be done with feet (the humor of anticlimax, but suggesting a return to
normality)   95 *Merlin* (a legendary magician associated with King Arthur,
who reigned later than King Lear)

III, iii *Enter Gloucester and Edmund.*

GLOUCESTER Alack, alack, Edmund, I like not this unnatural dealing. When I desired their leave that I might
3 pity him, they took from me the use of mine own house,
charged me on pain of perpetual displeasure neither to
5 speak of him, entreat for him, or any way sustain him.

EDMUND Most savage and unnatural.

7 GLOUCESTER Go to; say you nothing. There is division
8 between the Dukes, and a worse matter than that. I have
received a letter this night – 'tis dangerous to be spoken
10 – I have locked the letter in my closet. These injuries the
11 King now bears will be revenged home; there is part of a
12 power already footed; we must incline to the King. I will
13 look him and privily relieve him. Go you and maintain
talk with the Duke, that my charity be not of him perceived. If he ask for me, I am ill and gone to bed. If I die
for it, as no less is threatened me, the King my old mas-
17 ter must be relieved. There is strange things toward,
Edmund; pray you be careful.   *Exit.*

EDMUND
19 This courtesy forbid thee shall the Duke
Instantly know, and of that letter too.
21 This seems a fair deserving, and must draw me
That which my father loses – no less than all.
The younger rises when the old doth fall.   *Exit.*

*

III, iv *Enter Lear, Kent, and Fool.*

KENT
1 Here is the place, my lord. Good my lord, enter.
The tyranny of the open night's too rough

III, iii Within Gloucester's castle 3 *pity* have mercy upon 5 *entreat*
plead 7 *division* contention 8 *worse* more serious 10 *closet* chamber
11 *home* thoroughly 12 *power* army; *footed* landed; *incline to* side with
13 *look* search for; *privily* secretly 17 *toward* imminent 19 *courtesy* kind
attention (to Lear) 21 *fair deserving* i.e. action that should win favor
III, iv Before a hovel on the heath 1 *Good my lord* my good lord

For nature to endure.
    Storm still.

LEAR   Let me alone.

KENT
  Good my lord, enter here.

LEAR   Wilt break my heart?   4

KENT
  I had rather break mine own. Good my lord, enter.

LEAR
  Thou think'st 'tis much that this contentious storm
  Invades us to the skin. So 'tis to thee,
  But where the greater malady is fixed   8
  The lesser is scarce felt. Thou'dst shun a bear;
  But if thy flight lay toward the roaring sea,
  Thou'dst meet the bear i' th' mouth. When the mind's 11
    free,
  The body's delicate. The tempest in my mind
  Doth from my senses take all feeling else
  Save what beats there. Filial ingratitude,
  Is it not as this mouth should tear this hand
  For lifting food to't? But I will punish home.   16
  No, I will weep no more. In such a night
  To shut me out! Pour on; I will endure.
  In such a night as this! O Regan, Goneril,
  Your old kind father, whose frank heart gave all – 20
  O, that way madness lies; let me shun that.
  No more of that.

KENT   Good my lord, enter here.

LEAR
  Prithee go in thyself; seek thine own ease.
  This tempest will not give me leave to ponder
  On things would hurt me more, but I'll go in.
    [To the Fool]
  In, boy; go first. You houseless poverty –   26

---

4 *break my heart* i.e. by removing the distraction of mere physical distress
8 *fixed* lodged   11 *i' th' mouth* i.e. in the teeth; *free* free of care   16 *home*
i.e. to the hilt   20 *frank* liberal   26 *houseless* unsheltered

Nay, get thee in. I'll pray, and then I'll sleep. *Exit [Fool]*.
Poor naked wretches, wheresoe'er you are,
That bide the pelting of this pitiless storm,
How shall your houseless heads and unfed sides,
31   Your looped and windowed raggedness, defend you
From seasons such as these ? O, I have ta'en
33   Too little care of this ! Take physic, pomp ;
Expose thyself to feel what wretches feel,
35   That thou mayst shake the superflux to them
And show the heavens more just.

37 EDGAR *[within]* Fathom and half, fathom and half ! Poor
Tom !
    Enter Fool.

FOOL Come not in here, nuncle ; here's a spirit. Help me,
help me !

KENT
Give me thy hand. Who's there ?

FOOL A spirit, a spirit. He says his name 's poor Tom.

KENT
What art thou that dost grumble there i' th' straw ?
Come forth.
    Enter Edgar [as Tom o' Bedlam].

45 EDGAR Away ! the foul fiend follows me. Through the
46   sharp hawthorn blow the winds. Humh ! go to thy bed
and warm thee.

LEAR Didst thou give all to thy daughters ? And art thou
come to this ?

EDGAR Who gives anything to poor Tom ? whom the foul
fiend hath led through fire and through flame, through
ford and whirlpool, o'er bog and quagmire ; that hath
53   laid knives under his pillow and halters in his pew, set
54   ratsbane by his porridge, made him proud of heart, to

---

31 *looped* loopholed 33 *Take physic, pomp* i.e. cure yourself, you vain-
glorious ones 35 *superflux* superfluities 37 *Fathom and half* (nautical
cry in taking soundings, perhaps suggested by the deluge) 45–46 *Through
. . . winds* (cf. ll. 93–94; a line from a ballad) 46–47 *go . . . thee* (evidently a
popular retort; cf. *Taming of the Shrew*, Ind., i, 7–8) 53, 54 *knives
halters, ratsbane* (temptations to suicide) 53 *pew* a gallery or balcony

ride on a bay trotting horse over four-inched bridges, to 55
course his own shadow for a traitor. Bless thy five wits, 56
Tom 's acold. O, do, de, do, de, do, de. Bless thee from
whirlwinds, star-blasting, and taking. Do poor Tom 58
some charity, whom the foul fiend vexes. There could I
have him now – and there – and there again – and there –
    Storm still.

LEAR
Has his daughters brought him to this pass ?   61
Couldst thou save nothing ? Wouldst thou give 'em all ?

FOOL Nay, he reserved a blanket, else we had been all 63
shamed.

LEAR
Now all the plagues that in the pendulous air   65
Hang fated o'er men's faults light on thy daughters ! 66

KENT
He hath no daughters, sir.

LEAR
Death, traitor ! Nothing could have subdued nature
To such a lowness but his unkind daughters.
Is it the fashion that discarded fathers
Should have thus little mercy on their flesh ?   71
Judicious punishment – 'twas this flesh begot
Those pelican daughters.   73

EDGAR Pillicock sat on Pillicock Hill. Alow, alow, loo, loo ! 74

FOOL This cold night will turn us all to fools and madmen.

EDGAR Take heed o' th' foul fiend ; obey thy parents ;
    keep thy words' justice ; swear not ; commit not with 77

---

55 *ride . . . bridges* i.e. take mad risks   56 *course . . . traitor* chase his own
shadow as an enemy   58 *star-blasting* i.e. becoming the victim of malig-
nant stars ; *taking* pestilence   61 *pass* evil condition   63 *blanket* (to cover
his nakedness)   65 *pendulous* ominously suspended   66 *Hang . . . faults*
i.e. destined to chastise sins   71 *have . . . flesh* i.e. torture themselves   73
pelican i.e. feeding upon the parent's blood (a supposed habit of this
species of bird)   74 *Pillicock . . . Hill* (probably from a nursery rhyme ;
'Pillicock' is a pet name for a child) ; *Alow . . . loo* (hunting cry ?)   77
justice i.e. dependability ; *commit not* (i.e. adultery)

man's sworn spouse; set not thy sweet heart on proud
array. Tom's acold.

LEAR What hast thou been?

EDGAR A servingman, proud in heart and mind; that
82 curled my hair, wore gloves in my cap; served the lust of
my mistress' heart, and did the act of darkness with her;
swore as many oaths as I spake words, and broke them in
the sweet face of heaven. One that slept in the contriving
of lust, and waked to do it. Wine loved I deeply, dice
87 dearly; and in woman out-paramoured the Turk. False
88 of heart, light of ear, bloody of hand; hog in sloth, fox in
stealth, wolf in greediness, dog in madness, lion in prey.
90 Let not the creaking of shoes nor the rustling of silks be-
tray thy poor heart to woman. Keep thy foot out of
92 brothels, thy hand out of plackets, thy pen from lenders'
books, and defy the foul fiend. Still through the haw-
94 thorn blows the cold wind; says suum, mun, nonny.
95 Dolphin my boy, boy, sessa! let him trot by.
      Storm still.

96 LEAR Thou wert better in a grave than to answer with thy
uncovered body this extremity of the skies. Is man no
98 more than this? Consider him well. Thou ow'st the
worm no silk, the beast no hide, the sheep no wool, the
100 cat no perfume. Ha! here's three on's are sophisticated.
101 Thou art the thing itself; unaccommodated man is no
102 more but such a poor, bare, forked animal as thou art.
103 Off, off, you lendings! Come, unbutton here.
      [Begins to disrobe.]

---

82 *gloves . . . cap* (a fashion among Elizabethan gallants) 87 *out-
paramoured the Turk* outdid the Sultan in mistress-keeping 88 *light of
ear* i.e. attentive to flattery and slander 90 *creaking, rustling* (both
considered seductively fashionable sounds) 92 *plackets* slits in skirts
92–93 *pen . . . books* (in signing for loans) 94 *suum . . . nonny* (the refrain
of the wind?) 95 *Dolphin . . . trot by* (variously explained as cant phrases
or ballad refrain, equivalent to 'Let it go') 96 *answer* bear the brunt of
98 *ow'st* have borrowed from 100 *cat* civet cat; *sophisticated* altered by
artifice 101 *unaccommodated* unpampered 102 *forked* two-legged 103
lendings borrowed coverings

FOOL Prithee, nuncle, be contented; 'tis a naughty night 104
to swim in. Now a little fire in a wild field were like an 105
old lecher's heart – a small spark, all the rest on's body
cold. Look, here comes a walking fire.
        Enter Gloucester with a torch.

EDGAR This is the foul Flibbertigibbet. He begins at cur- 108
few, and walks till the first cock. He gives the web and 109
the pin, squints the eye, and makes the harelip; mildews 110
the white wheat, and hurts the poor creature of earth. 111
            Swithold footed thrice the 'old; 112
            He met the nightmare, and her nine fold; 113
            Bid her alight 114
            And her troth plight, 115
        And aroint thee, witch, aroint thee! 116

KENT
    How fares your Grace?

LEAR What's he?

KENT
    Who's there? What is't you seek?

GLOUCESTER
    What are you there? Your names?

EDGAR Poor Tom, that eats the swimming frog, the toad,
the todpole, the wall-newt and the water; that in the fury 122
of his heart, when the foul fiend rages, eats cow-dung
for sallets, swallows the old rat and the ditch-dog, drinks 124
the green mantle of the standing pool; who is whipped 125
from tithing to tithing, and stock-punished and im- 126
prisoned; who hath had three suits to his back, six

---

104 *naughty* evil   105 *wild* barren   108 *Flibbertigibbet* (a dancing devil);
curfew (9 p.m.)   109 *first cock* (midnight)   109–10 *web . . . pin* cataract of
the eye   110 *squints* crosses   111 *white* ripening   112 *Swithold* St Withold
(Anglo-Saxon exorcist); *footed* walked over; *'old* wold, uplands   113
nightmare incubus, demon; *fold* offspring   114 *alight* i.e. from the horse
she was afflicting   115 *her troth plight* plight her troth, pledge her good
intentions   116 *aroint thee* be gone (a direct command, concluding the
charm)   122 *todpole* tadpole; *water* water-newt   124 *sallets* salads; *ditch-
dog* (carcass)   125 *mantle* scum; *standing* stagnant   126 *tithing* a ten-
family district within a parish; *stock-punished* placed in the stocks

shirts to his body,
>   Horse to ride, and weapon to wear,
130   But mice and rats, and such small deer,
>   Have been Tom's food for seven long year.

132   Beware my follower! Peace, Smulkin, peace, thou fiend!

GLOUCESTER
What, hath your Grace no better company?

EDGAR
The prince of darkness is a gentleman.
135   Modo he's called, and Mahu.

GLOUCESTER
Our flesh and blood, my lord, is grown so vile
137   That it doth hate what gets it.

EDGAR Poor Tom's acold.

GLOUCESTER
139   Go in with me. My duty cannot suffer
T' obey in all your daughters' hard commands.
Though their injunction be to bar my doors
And let this tyrannous night take hold upon you,
Yet have I ventured to come seek you out
And bring you where both fire and food is ready.

LEAR
First let me talk with this philosopher.
What is the cause of thunder?

KENT
Good my lord, take his offer; go into th' house.

LEAR
148   I'll talk a word with this same learnèd Theban.
149   What is your study?

EDGAR
150   How to prevent the fiend, and to kill vermin.

---

130 *deer* game (adapted from lines in the romance *Bevis of Hampton*) 132, 135 *Smulkin, Modo, Mahu* (devils described in Harsnett's *Declaration*, 1603) 137 *gets* begets (a reference to Edgar, Goneril, and Regan) 139 *suffer* permit 148 *Theban* (an unexplained association of Thebes with philosophy, i.e. science) 149 *study* i.e. scientific specialty 150 *prevent* thwart

LEAR
Let me ask you one word in private.

KENT
Importune him once more to go, my lord.
His wits begin t' unsettle.

GLOUCESTER   Canst thou blame him?
        Storm still.
His daughters seek his death. Ah, that good Kent,
He said it would be thus, poor banished man!
Thou sayest the King grows mad – I'll tell thee, friend,
I am almost mad myself. I had a son,
Now outlawed from my blood; he sought my life   158
But lately, very late. I loved him, friend,
No father his son dearer. True to tell thee,
The grief hath crazed my wits. What a night's this!
I do beseech your Grace –

LEAR   O, cry you mercy, sir.   162
Noble philosopher, your company.

EDGAR Tom's acold.

GLOUCESTER
In, fellow, there, into th' hovel; keep thee warm.

LEAR
Come, let's in all.

KENT   This way, my lord.

LEAR   With him!
I will keep still with my philosopher.

KENT
Good my lord, soothe him; let him take the fellow.   168

GLOUCESTER
Take him you on.   169

KENT
Sirrah, come on; go along with us.

LEAR
Come, good Athenian.   171

---

158 *outlawed . . . blood* proscribed as no child of mine   **162** *cry you mercy*
I beg your pardon   **168** *soothe* humor   **169** *you on* along with you   **171**
Athenian i.e. philosopher

GLOUCESTER
No words, no words! Hush.

173 EDGAR   Child Rowland to the dark tower came;
174   His word was still, 'Fie, foh, and fum,
             I smell the blood of a British man.'   *Exeunt.*

*

III, v   *Enter Cornwall and Edmund.*

CORNWALL I will have my revenge ere I depart his house.

2 EDMUND How, my lord, I may be censured, that nature
3   thus gives way to loyalty, something fears me to think of.

CORNWALL I now perceive it was not altogether your
5   brother's evil disposition made him seek his death; but a
     provoking merit, set awork by a reproveable badness in
     himself.

EDMUND How malicious is my fortune that I must repent
     to be just! This is the letter which he spoke of, which
10   approves him an intelligent party to the advantages of
     France. O heavens, that this treason were not! or not I
     the detector!

CORNWALL Go with me to the Duchess.

EDMUND If the matter of this paper be certain, you have
     mighty business in hand.

CORNWALL True or false, it hath made thee Earl of
     Gloucester. Seek out where thy father is, that he may be
     ready for our apprehension.

19 EDMUND *[aside]* If I find him comforting the King, it
20   will stuff his suspicion more fully. – I will persever in

173 *Child* (i.e. a candidate for knighthood); *Rowland* Roland of the Charle-
magne legends (the line perhaps from a lost ballad) 174 *His word was
still* i.e. his repeated word, his motto, was always 174–75 *Fie . . . man*
(absurdly heroic)
III, v Within Gloucester's castle 2 *censured* judged 3 *something fears me*
frightens me somewhat 5–7 *a provoking . . . himself* i.e. evil justice incited
by evil (a case of poison driving out poison) 10 *approves* proves; *intelligent . . . advantages* spying partisan on behalf 19 *comforting* aiding
20 *persever* persevere

my course of loyalty, though the conflict be sore between that and my blood.   22
CORNWALL I will lay trust upon thee, and thou shalt find 23
a dearer father in my love.   *Exeunt*.

*

Enter Kent and Gloucester.   III, vi
GLOUCESTER Here is better than the open air; take it
thankfully. I will piece out the comfort with what addition I can. I will not be long from you.
KENT All the power of his wits have given way to his
impatience. The gods reward your kindness.   5
                                    Exit [Gloucester].
Enter Lear, Edgar, and Fool.
EDGAR Frateretto calls me, and tells me Nero is an angler 6
in the lake of darkness. Pray, innocent, and beware the 7
foul fiend.
FOOL Prithee, nuncle, tell me whether a madman be a
gentleman or a yeoman.   10
LEAR
A king, a king.
FOOL No, he's a yeoman that has a gentleman to his son;
for he's a mad yeoman that sees his son a gentleman 13
before him.
LEAR
To have a thousand with red burning spits
Come hizzing in upon 'em –   16
[EDGAR The foul fiend bites my back.

---

22 *blood* natural feelings **23** *lay . . . thee* trust you (?), reward you with
a place of trust (?)
III, vi Within a cottage near Gloucester's castle **5** *impatience* rage
6 *Frateretto* (a devil mentioned in Harsnett's *Declaration*); *Nero* (in
Rabelais, Trajan was the angler, Nero a fiddler, in Hades) **7** *innocent*
hapless victim, plaything **10** *yeoman* a property owner, next in rank to
a gentleman (The allusion is to self-penalizing indulgence of one's children.)
13 *sees* i.e. sees to it **16** *hizzing* hissing (Lear is musing on vicious military
retaliation)

FOOL He's mad that trusts in the tameness of a wolf, a
horse's health, a boy's love, or a whore's oath.

LEAR

20   It shall be done; I will arraign them straight.
            [To Edgar]
      Come, sit thou here, most learned justice.
            [To the Fool]
      Thou, sapient sir, sit here. Now, you she-foxes –

23 EDGAR Look, where he stands and glares. Want'st thou
24   eyes at trial, madam?

25   Come o'er the bourn, Bessy, to me.

      FOOL   Her boat hath a leak,
                      And she must not speak
                  Why she dares not come over to thee.

EDGAR The foul fiend haunts poor Tom in the voice of a
30   nightingale. Hoppedance cries in Tom's belly for two
31   white herring. Croak not, black angel; I have no food
      for thee.

KENT

33   How do you, sir? Stand you not so amazed.
      Will you lie down and rest upon the cushions?

LEAR

      I'll see their trial first. Bring in their evidence.
            [To Edgar]
      Thou, robèd man of justice, take thy place.
            [To the Fool]
      And thou, his yokefellow of equity,
38   Bench by his side. *[to Kent]* You are o' th' commission;
      Sit you too.

EDGAR Let us deal justly.

---

20 *arraign* bring to trial   **23** *he* Lear (?), one of Edgar's 'devils' (?)   **24**
eyes such eyes (?), spectators (?)   **25** *bourn* brook (Edgar's line is from a
popular song; the Fool's are a ribald improvisation)   **30** *nightingale* i.e.
the fool; *Hoppedance* (a devil mentioned in Harsnett's *Declaration* as
'Hobberdidance')   **31** *white* unsmoked (in contrast with *black angel*, i.e.
smoked devil)   **33** *amazed* bewildered   **38** *commission* those commissioned
as King's justices

    Sleepest or wakest thou, jolly shepherd?
        Thy sheep be in the corn;   42
    And for one blast of thy minikin mouth   43
        Thy sheep shall take no harm.
Purr, the cat is gray.   45

LEAR Arraign her first. 'Tis Goneril, I here take my oath before this honorable assembly, kicked the poor king her father.

FOOL Come hither, mistress. Is your name Goneril?

LEAR She cannot deny it.

FOOL Cry you mercy, I took you for a joint-stool.   51

LEAR
    And here's another, whose warped looks proclaim
    What store her heart is made on. Stop her there!
    Arms, arms, sword, fire! Corruption in the place!   54
    False justicer, why hast thou let her 'scape?]

EDGAR Bless thy five wits!

KENT
    O pity! Sir, where is the patience now
    That you so oft have boasted to retain?

EDGAR [aside]
    My tears begin to take his part so much   59
    They mar my counterfeiting.   60

LEAR
    The little dogs and all,
    Tray, Blanch, and Sweetheart – see, they bark at me.

EDGAR Tom will throw his head at them. Avaunt, you curs.
        Be thy mouth or black or white,
        Tooth that poisons if it bite;
        Mastiff, greyhound, mongrel grim,

---

42 *corn* wheatfield **43** *one . . . mouth* one strain on your delicate shepherd's pipe (?) **45** *gray* (gray cats were among the forms supposedly assumed by devils) **51** *Cry . . . joint-stool* (a cant expression for 'Pardon me for failing to notice you,' but two joint-stools – cf. *warped*, l. 52 – were probably the actual stage objects arraigned as Goneril and Regan) **54** *Corruption . . . place* i.e. bribery in the court **59** *takes his part* i.e. fall on his behalf **60** *counterfeiting* i.e. simulating madness

67   Hound or spaniel, brach or lym,
68   Or bobtail tike, or trundle-tail –
              Tom will make him weep and wail;
              For, with throwing thus my head,
71   Dogs leaped the hatch, and all are fled.
72 Do, de, de, de. Sessa! Come, march to wakes and fairs
73 and market towns. Poor Tom, thy horn is dry.

LEAR Then let them anatomize Regan. See what breeds
about her heart. Is there any cause in nature that makes
these hard hearts? *[to Edgar]* You, sir, I entertain for
one of my hundred; only I do not like the fashion of
78 your garments. You will say they are Persian; but let
them be changed.

KENT
Now, good my lord, lie here and rest awhile.

LEAR
Make no noise, make no noise; draw the curtains.
So, so. We'll go to supper i' th' morning.

FOOL And I'll go to bed at noon.

       Enter Gloucester.

GLOUCESTER
Come hither, friend. Where is the King my master?

KENT
Here, sir, but trouble him not; his wits are gone.

GLOUCESTER
Good friend, I prithee take him in thy arms.
I have o'erheard a plot of death upon him.
There is a litter ready; lay him in't
And drive toward Dover, friend, where thou shalt meet
Both welcome and protection. Take up thy master.
If thou shouldst dally half an hour, his life,

---

67 *brach* hound bitch; *lym* bloodhound   68 *bobtail . . . trundle-tail* short-
tailed cur or long-tailed 71 *hatch* lower half of a 'Dutch door' 72 *Sessa*
(interjection, equivalent to 'Away!'); *wakes* parish feasts 73 *Poor . . . dry*
(Edgar expresses his exhaustion in his role, by an allusion to the horns
proffered by Toms o' Bedlam in begging drink) 78 *Persian* (Persian cos-
tume was reputedly gorgeous. Ironically, or in actual delusion, Lear refers
thus to Edgar's rags, as he refers to bed curtains in l. 81.)

With thine and all that offer to defend him,
Stand in assurèd loss. Take up, take up,
And follow me, that will to some provision   94
Give thee quick conduct.   95
[KENT   Oppressèd nature sleeps.
This rest might yet have balmed thy broken sinews,   96
Which, if convenience will not allow,   97
Stand in hard cure.   98
    [To the Fool] Come, help to bear thy master.
Thou must not stay behind.]
GLOUCESTER   Come, come, away!
              Exeunt [all but Edgar].

[EDGAR
When we our betters see bearing our woes,   100
We scarcely think our miseries our foes.   101
Who alone suffers suffers most i' th' mind,
Leaving free things and happy shows behind;   103
But then the mind much sufferance doth o'erskip   104
When grief hath mates, and bearing fellowship.   105
How light and portable my pain seems now,   106
When that which makes me bend makes the King bow.
He childed as I fatherèd. Tom, away.
Mark the high noises, and thyself bewray   109
When false opinion, whose wrong thoughts defile thee,   110
In thy just proof repeals and reconciles thee.   111
What will hap more to-night, safe 'scape the King!   112
Lurk, lurk.]   *[Exit.]*   113

                        *

94 *provision* supplies   95 *conduct* guidance   96 *balmed* healed; *sinews* nerves   97 *convenience* propitious circumstances   98 *Stand . . . cure* will be hard to cure   100 *our woes* woes like ours   101 *our foes* i.e. our peculiar foes (they seem rather a part of universal misery)   103 *free* carefree; *shows* scenes   104 *sufferance* suffering   105 *bearing fellowship* enduring has company   106 *portable* bearable   109 *Mark . . . noises* i.e. heed the rumors concerning those in power (?); *bewray* reveal   110 *wrong thoughts* misconceptions   111 *In . . . reconciles thee* i.e. upon your vindication recalls you and makes peace with you   112 *What . . . more* whatever more happens   113 *Lurk* i.e. keep covered

III, vii   *Enter Cornwall, Regan, Goneril, Bastard [Edmund],*
and Servants.

CORNWALL *[to Goneril]* Post speedily to my lord your
husband; show him this letter. The army of France is
landed. *[to Servants]* Seek out the traitor Gloucester.
[Exeunt some Servants.]

REGAN Hang him instantly.

GONERIL Pluck out his eyes.

CORNWALL Leave him to my displeasure. Edmund, keep
7   you our sister company. The revenges we are bound to
take upon your traitorous father are not fit for your be-
holding. Advise the Duke where you are going, to a most
10   festinate preparation. We are bound to the like. Our
11   posts shall be swift and intelligent betwixt us. Farewell,
12   dear sister; farewell, my Lord of Gloucester.
Enter Steward [Oswald].
How now? Where's the King?

OSWALD
My Lord of Gloucester hath conveyed him hence.
Some five or six and thirty of his knights,
16   Hot questrists after him, met him at gate;
Who, with some other of the lord's dependants,
Are gone with him toward Dover, where they boast
To have well-armèd friends.

CORNWALL   Get horses for your mistress.
Exit [Oswald].

GONERIL
Farewell, sweet lord, and sister.

CORNWALL
Edmund, farewell.   *[Exeunt Goneril and Edmund.]*
Go seek the traitor Gloucester,
Pinion him like a thief, bring him before us.
[Exeunt other Servants.]

III, vii Within Gloucester's castle   7 *bound* required   10 *festinate* speedy
11 *intelligent* informative   12 *Lord of Gloucester* (as now endowed with
his father's title and estates)   16 *questrists* seekers

Though well we may not pass upon his life   23
Without the form of justice, yet our power
Shall do a court'sy to our wrath, which men   25
May blame, but not control.
    Enter Gloucester and Servants.
                  Who's there, the traitor?

REGAN
Ingrateful fox, 'tis he.

CORNWALL
Bind fast his corky arms.   28

GLOUCESTER
What means your Graces? Good my friends, consider
You are my guests. Do me no foul play, friends.

CORNWALL
Bind him, I say.
    [Servants bind him.]
REGAN   Hard, hard! O filthy traitor.

GLOUCESTER
Unmerciful lady as you are, I'm none.

CORNWALL
To this chair bind him. Villain, thou shalt find –
    [Regan plucks his beard.]

GLOUCESTER
By the kind gods, 'tis most ignobly done
To pluck me by the beard.

REGAN
So white, and such a traitor?

GLOUCESTER   Naughty lady,   36
These hairs which thou dost ravish from my chin
Will quicken and accuse thee. I am your host.   38
With robber's hands my hospitable favors   39
You should not ruffle thus. What will you do?   40

CORNWALL
Come, sir, what letters had you late from France?   41

---

23 *pass upon* issue a sentence against   **25** *do a court'sy to* i.e. defer to, act in
conformity with   **28** *corky* (because aged)   **36** *Naughty* evil   **38** *quicken*
come to life   **39** *favors* features   **40** *ruffle* tear at   **41** *late* of late

REGAN

42   Be simple-answered, for we know the truth.

CORNWALL

And what confederacy have you with the traitors

44   Late footed in the kingdom?

REGAN

To whose hands you have sent the lunatic King.
Speak.

GLOUCESTER

47   I have a letter guessingly set down,
Which came from one that's of a neutral heart,
And not from one opposed.

CORNWALL   Cunning.

REGAN   And false.

CORNWALL

Where hast thou sent the king?

GLOUCESTER

To Dover.

REGAN

52   Wherefore to Dover? Wast thou not charged at peril –

CORNWALL

Wherefore to Dover? Let him answer that.

GLOUCESTER

54   I am tied to th' stake, and I must stand the course.

REGAN

Wherefore to Dover?

GLOUCESTER

Because I would not see thy cruel nails
Pluck out his poor old eyes; nor thy fierce sister

58   In his anointed flesh stick boarish fangs.
The sea, with such a storm as his bare head

60   In hell-black night endured, would have buoyed up

---

42 *Be simple-answered* i.e. give plain answers 44 *footed* landed 47
guessingly i.e. tentatively, not stated as an assured fact 52 *charged at peril*
ordered on peril of your life 54 *course* coursing (as by a string of dogs
baiting a bear or bull tied in the pit) 58 *anointed* (as king) 60 *buoyed*
surged

And quenched the stellèd fires.   61
Yet, poor old heart, he holp the heavens to rain.   62
If wolves had at thy gate howled that stern time,
Thou shouldst have said, 'Good porter, turn the key.'   64
All cruels else subscribe. But I shall see   65
The wingèd vengeance overtake such children.   66

CORNWALL
See't shalt thou never. Fellows, hold the chair.
Upon these eyes of thine I'll set my foot.

GLOUCESTER
He that will think to live till he be old,   69
Give me some help. – O cruel! O you gods!

REGAN
One side will mock another. Th' other too.   71

CORNWALL
If you see vengeance –

1. SERVANT   Hold your hand, my lord!
I have served you ever since I was a child;
But better service have I never done you
Than now to bid you hold.

REGAN   How now, you dog?

1. SERVANT
If you did wear a beard upon your chin,
I'ld shake it on this quarrel. What do you mean!   77

CORNWALL
My villain!   78
        [Draw and fight.]

1. SERVANT
Nay, then, come on, and take the chance of anger.

---

61 *stellèd* starry   **62** *holp* helped   **64** *turn the key* i.e. let them come in to shelter   **65** *All . . . subscribe* i.e. at such times all other cruel creatures give way, agree to renounce their cruelty (?)   **66** *wingèd* heavenly (?), swift (?)   **69** *will think* hopes, expects   **71** *mock* i.e. subject to ridicule (because of the contrast)   **77** *shake it* (as Regan has done with Gloucester's – an act of extreme defiance); *on this quarrel* in this cause; *What . . . mean* i.e. how dare you (The words are given to Regan by most editors, but they are no more 'un-servantlike,' than those which precede them.)   **78** *My villain* i.e. my serf (with play on its more modern meaning)

REGAN
   Give me thy sword. A peasant stand up thus?
       [She takes a sword and runs at him behind,] kills him.

1. SERVANT
   O, I am slain! My lord, you have one eye left
82 To see some mischief on him. O!

CORNWALL
   Lest it see more, prevent it. Out, vile jelly.
   Where is thy lustre now?

GLOUCESTER
   All dark and comfortless. Where's my son Edmund?
86 Edmund, enkindle all the sparks of nature
87 To quit this horrid act.

REGAN   Out, treacherous villain;
   Thou call'st on him that hates thee. It was he
89 That made the overture of thy treasons to us;
   Who is too good to pity thee.

GLOUCESTER
91 O my follies! Then Edgar was abused.
   Kind gods, forgive me that, and prosper him.

REGAN
   Go thrust him out at gates, and let him smell
   His way to Dover.   *Exit [one] with Gloucester.*
94   How is't, my lord? How look you?

CORNWALL
   I have received a hurt. Follow me, lady.
   Turn out that eyeless villain. Throw this slave
   Upon the dunghill. Regan, I bleed apace.
   Untimely comes this hurt. Give me your arm.   *Exeunt.*

[2. SERVANT
   I'll never care what wickedness I do,
   If this man come to good.

3. SERVANT   If she live long,

82 *mischief* injury   86 *nature* natural feeling   87 *quit* requite, avenge;
horrid horrible   89 *overture* disclosure   91 *abused* wronged   94 *How look
you* i.e. how looks it with you, what is your condition

And in the end meet the old course of death,   101
Women will all turn monsters.

2 . SERVANT
Let's follow the old Earl, and get the bedlam
To lead him where he would. His roguish madness   104
Allows itself to anything.   *[Exit.]*

3 . SERVANT
Go thou. I'll fetch some flax and whites of eggs
To apply to his bleeding face. Now heaven help him.
                                                    Exit.]

*

Enter Edgar.   IV, i

EDGAR
Yet better thus, and known to be contemned,   1
Than still contemned and flattered. To be worst,
The lowest and most dejected thing of fortune,   3
Stands still in esperance, lives not in fear.   4
The lamentable change is from the best;
The worst returns to laughter. Welcome then,   6
Thou unsubstantial air that I embrace:
The wretch that thou hast blown unto the worst
Owes nothing to thy blasts.   9
      Enter Gloucester and an Old Man.
                              But who comes here?
My father, poorly led? World, world, O world!   10
But that thy strange mutations make us hate thee,   11
Life would not yield to age.

OLD MAN   O my good lord,
I have been your tenant, and your father's tenant,
These fourscore years.

---

101 *meet . . . death* i.e. die a natural death   104–05 *His roguish . . . anything*
i.e. his being an irresponsible wanderer allows him to do anything
IV, i A path leading from Gloucester's castle   1 *contemned* despised   3
dejected cast down, abased   4 *esperance* hope   6 *The worst . . . laughter* i.e.
the worst extreme is the point of return to liappiness   9 *nothing* i.e. nothing
good (and hence he is free of debt)   10 *poorly* poor-like, i.e. like a blind
beggar (?)   11–12 *But . . . age* i.e. were it not for your hateful mutability,
we would never be reconciled to old age and death

GLOUCESTER
Away, get thee away. Good friend, be gone.
16 Thy comforts can do me no good at all;
17 Thee they may hurt.
OLD MAN   You cannot see your way.
GLOUCESTER
18 I have no way, and therefore want no eyes;
I stumbled when I saw. Full oft 'tis seen
20 Our means secure us, and our mere defects
Prove our commodities. O dear son Edgar,
22 The food of thy abusèd father's wrath,
23 Might I but live to see thee in my touch
I'ld say I had eyes again!
OLD MAN   How now? Who's there?
EDGAR [aside]
O gods! Who is't can say 'I am at the worst'?
I am worse than e'er I was.
OLD MAN   'Tis poor mad Tom.
EDGAR [aside]
27 And worse I may be yet. The worst is not
So long as we can say 'This is the worst.'
OLD MAN
Fellow, where goest?
GLOUCESTER   Is it a beggarman?
OLD MAN
Madman and beggar too.
GLOUCESTER
31 He has some reason, else he could not beg.
I' th' last night's storm I such a fellow saw,
33 Which made me think a man a worm. My son

---

16 *comforts* ministrations   17 *hurt* do injury (since they are forbidden)
18 *want* need   20–21 *Our means . . . commodities* i.e. prosperity makes us
rash, and sheer affliction proves a boon   22 *food* i.e. the object fed upon;
abusèd deceived   23 *in* i.e. by means of   27–28 *The worst . . . worst* (because
at the very worst there will be no such comforting thought)   31 *reason*
powers of reason   33–34 *My son . . . mind* (because it was actually he —
a natural touch)

Came then into my mind, and yet my mind
Was then scarce friends with him. I have heard more
    since.
As flies to wanton boys are we to th' gods;   36
They kill us for their sport.

EDGAR [aside]   How should this be?
Bad is the trade that must play fool to sorrow,
Ang'ring itself and others. – Bless thee, master.   39

GLOUCESTER
Is that the naked fellow?

OLD MAN   Ay, my lord.

GLOUCESTER
Then prithee get thee gone. If for my sake
Thou wilt o'ertake us hence a mile or twain
I' th' way toward Dover, do it for ancient love;   43
And bring some covering for this naked soul,
Which I'll entreat to lead me.

OLD MAN   Alack, sir, he is mad.

GLOUCESTER
'Tis the time's plague when madmen lead the blind.   46
Do as I bid thee, or rather do thy pleasure.   47
Above the rest, be gone.

OLD MAN
I'll bring him the best 'parel that I have,   49
Come on't what will.   Exit.

GLOUCESTER
Sirrah naked fellow –

EDGAR
Poor Tom's acold. [aside] I cannot daub it further.   52

GLOUCESTER
Come hither, fellow.

EDGAR [aside]
And yet I must. – Bless thy sweet eyes, they bleed.

---

36 *wanton* irresponsibly playful   **39** *Ang'ring* offending   **43** *ancient love*
i.e. such love as formerly bound master and man (nostalgic)   **46** *time's
plague* i.e. malady characteristic of these times   **47** *thy pleasure* as you
please   **49** *'parel* apparel   **52** *daub it* lay it on, act the part

GLOUCESTER
Know'st thou the way to Dover?

EDGAR Both stile and gate, horseway and footpath. Poor
Tom hath been scared out of his good wits. Bless thee,
good man's son, from the foul fiend. [Five fiends have
59　　been in poor Tom at once: of lust, as Obidicut; Hobbi-
60　　didence, prince of dumbness; Mahu, of stealing; Modo,
61　　of murder; Flibbertigibbet, of mopping and mowing,
who since possesses chambermaids and waiting women.
So, bless thee, master.]

GLOUCESTER
Here, take this purse, thou whom the heavens' plagues
65　　Have humbled to all strokes. That I am wretched
66　　Makes thee the happier. Heavens, deal so still!
67　　Let the superfluous and lust-dieted man,
68　　That slaves your ordinance, that will not see
Because he does not feel, feel your pow'r quickly;
So distribution should undo excess,
And each man have enough. Dost thou know Dover?

EDGAR Ay, master.

GLOUCESTER
73　　There is a cliff, whose high and bending head
74　　Looks fearfully in the confinèd deep.
Bring me but to the very brim of it,
And I'll repair the misery thou dost bear
With something rich about me. From that place
I shall no leading need.

EDGAR　　　　　　　　　Give me thy arm.
Poor Tom shall lead thee.　　　　　　　　*Exeunt.*

*

59 *Obidicut* Hoberdicut (a devil mentioned in Harsnett's *Declaration*, as are
the four following)　60 *dumbness* muteness (Shakespeare identifies each
devil with some form of possession)　61 *mopping and mowing* grimaces,
affected facial expressions　65 *humbled to* reduced to bearing humbly
66 *happier* i.e. less wretched　67 *superfluous* possessed of superfluities;
lust-dieted i.e. whose desires are feasted　68 *slaves your ordinance* sub-
ordinates your injunction (to share)　73 *bending* overhanging　74 *in . . .
deep* i.e. to the sea hemmed in below

Enter Goneril, Bastard [Edmund], and Steward   IV, ii
[Oswald].

GONERIL

Welcome, my lord. I marvel our mild husband

Not met us on the way.   2

    [To Oswald]   Now, where's your master?

OSWALD

Madam, within, but never man so changed.

I told him of the army that was landed :

He smiled at it. I told him you were coming :

His answer was, 'The worse.' Of Gloucester's treachery

And of the loyal service of his son

When I informed him, then he called me sot   8

And told me I had turned the wrong side out.

What most he should dislike seems pleasant to him ;

What like, offensive.   11

GONERIL *[to Edmund]* Then shall you go no further.

It is the cowish terror of his spirit,   12

That dares not undertake. He'll not feel wrongs   13

Which tie him to an answer. Our wishes on the way   14

May prove effects. Back, Edmund, to my brother.

Hasten his musters and conduct his pow'rs.   16

I must change names at home, and give the distaff   17

Into my husband's hands. This trusty servant

Shall pass between us. Ere long you are like to hear

(If you dare venture in your own behalf)

A mistress's command. Wear this. Spare speech.   21

    [Gives a favor.]

Decline your head. This kiss, if it durst speak,

Would stretch thy spirits up into the air.

IV, ii Before Albany's palace   **2** *Not met* has not met   **8** *sot* fool   **11** *What like* what he should like   **12** *cowish* cowardly   **13** *undertake* engage   **14** *an answer* retaliation   **14–15** *Our wishes . . . effects* i.e. our wishes, that you might supplant Albany, may materialize   **16** *musters* enlistments; *conduct his pow'rs* lead his army   **17** *change names* i.e. exchange the name of 'mistress' for 'master'; *distaff* spinning-staff (symbol of the housewife)   **21** *mistress's* (at present she plays the role of master, but, mated with Edmund, she would again *change names*)

24   Conceive, and fare thee well.

EDMUND
        Yours in the ranks of death.   *Exit.*

GONERIL   My most dear Gloucester.
        O, the difference of man and man :
        To thee a woman's services are due ;
28   My fool usurps my body.

OSWALD   Madam, here comes my lord.
                                                    [*Exit.*]

        Enter Albany.

GONERIL
29   I have been worth the whistle.

ALBANY   O Goneril,
        You are not worth the dust which the rude wind
31   Blows in your face. [I fear your disposition :
        That nature which contemns its origin
33   Cannot be borderèd certain in itself.
34   She that herself will sliver and disbranch
35   From her material sap, perforce must wither
        And come to deadly use.

GONERIL
        No more ; the text is foolish.

ALBANY
        Wisdom and goodness to the vile seem vile ;
39   Filths savor but themselves. What have you done ?
        Tigers not daughters, what have you performed ?
        A father, and a gracious agèd man,
42   Whose reverence even the head-lugged bear would lick,
43   Most barbarous, most degenerate, have you madded.

24 *Conceive* (1) understand, (2) quicken (with the seed I have planted in
you)   28 *usurps* wrongfully occupies   29 *worth the whistle* i.e. valued
enough to be welcomed home ('not worth the whistle' applying proverbially
to a 'poor dog')   31 *fear your disposition* distrust your nature   33 *borderèd
certain* safely contained (it will be unpredictably licentious)   34 *sliver*,
disbranch cut off   35 *material sap* sustaining stock, nourishing trunk
39 *savor* relish   42 *head-lugged* dragged with a head-chain (hence, surly);
lick i.e. treat with affection   43 *degenerate* unnatural; *madded* maddened

Could my good brother suffer you to do it?
A man, a prince, by him so benefited!
If that the heavens do not their visible spirits   46
Send quickly down to tame these vile offenses,
It will come,   48
Humanity must perforce prey on itself,
Like monsters of the deep.]

GONERIL   Milk-livered man,   50
That bear'st a cheek for blows, a head for wrongs;
Who hast not in thy brows an eye discerning   52
Thine honor from thy suffering; [that not know'st
Fools do those villains pity who are punished   54
Ere they have done their mischief. Where's thy drum?   55
France spreads his banners in our noiseless land,   56
With plumèd helm thy state begins to threat,   57
Whilst thou, a moral fool, sits still and cries   58
'Alack, why does he so?']

ALBANY   See thyself, devil:
Proper deformity seems not in the fiend   60
So horrid as in woman.

GONERIL   O vain fool!

[ALBANY
Thou changèd and self-covered thing, for shame   62
Bemonster not thy feature. Were't my fitness   63
To let these hands obey my blood,   64
They are apt enough to dislocate and tear
Thy flesh and bones. Howe'er thou art a fiend,
A woman's shape doth shield thee.

---

46 *visible* made visible, material   48 *It* i.e. chaos   50 *Milk-livered* i.e.
spiritless   52–53 *discerning . . . suffering* distinguishing between dishonor
and tolerance   54 *Fools* i.e. only fools   55 *drum* i.e. military preparation   56 *noiseless* i.e. unaroused   57 *helm* war-helmet   58 *moral* moral-
izing   60 *Proper* i.e. fair-surfaced   62 *changèd* transformed (diabolically,
as in witchcraft); *self-covered* i.e. your natural self overwhelmed by
evil (?), devil disguised as woman (?)   63 *Bemonster . . . feature* i.e. do
not exchange your human features for a monster's; *my fitness* fit for me
64 *blood* passion

GONERIL
68   Marry, your manhood – mew !]
        Enter a Messenger.
[ALBANY   What news ?]
MESSENGER
     O, my good lord, the Duke of Cornwall's dead,
71   Slain by his servant, going to put out
     The other eye of Gloucester.
ALBANY   Gloucester's eyes ?
MESSENGER
73   A servant that he bred, thrilled with remorse,
     Opposed against the act, bending his sword
     To his great master ; who, thereat enraged,
76   Flew on him, and amongst them felled him dead ;
     But not without that harmful stroke which since
78   Hath plucked him after.
ALBANY   This shows you are above,
79   You justicers, that these our nether crimes
80   So speedily can venge. But, O poor Gloucester,
     Lost he his other eye ?
MESSENGER   Both, both, my lord.
82   This letter, madam, craves a speedy answer.
     'Tis from your sister.
GONERIL *[aside]*   One way I like this well ;
     But being widow, and my Gloucester with her,
85   May all the building in my fancy pluck
86   Upon my hateful life. Another way
87   The news is not so tart. – I'll read, and answer.   *[Exit.]*

---

68 *Marry* (oath, derived from 'By Mary'); *your manhood – mew* i.e. 'What a man!' followed by a contemptuous interjection (?), mew up (contain) this display of manliness (?)   71 *going to* about to   73 *bred* reared; *thrilled with remorse* in the throes of pity   76 *amongst them* i.e. aided by the others   78 *plucked him after* drawn him along (to death)   79 *justicers* dispensers of justice; *nether crimes* sins committed here below   80 *venge* avenge   82 *craves* requires   85–86 *May . . . life* i.e. may make my life hateful by destroying my dream-castles   86 *Another way* the other way (alluded to in l. 83, probably the removal of Cornwall as an obstacle to sole reign with Edmund)   87 *tart* distasteful

ALBANY
Where was his son when they did take his eyes?
MESSENGER
Come with my lady hither.
ALBANY   He is not here.
MESSENGER
No, my good lord; I met him back again.   90
ALBANY
Knows he the wickedness?
MESSENGER
Ay, my good lord. 'Twas he informed against him,
And quit the house on purpose, that their punishment
Might have the freer course.
ALBANY   Gloucester, I live
To thank thee for the love thou show'dst the King,
And to revenge thine eyes. Come hither, friend.
Tell me what more thou know'st.   *Exeunt.*

*

[*Enter Kent and a Gentleman.*   IV, iii
KENT Why the King of France is so suddenly gone back
    know you no reason?
GENTLEMAN Something he left imperfect in the state,   3
    which since his coming forth is thought of, which imports 4
    to the kingdom so much fear and danger that his per-   5
    sonal return was most required and necessary.   6
KENT
Who hath he left behind him general?
GENTLEMAN The Marshal of France, Monsieur La Far.
KENT Did your letters pierce the Queen to any demon-   9
    stration of grief?

90 *back* going back
IV, iii A meeting place at Dover   3 *imperfect . . . state* i.e. rift in affairs
of state   4 *imports* means   5 *fear* uneasiness   6 *most* most urgently
9 *pierce* goad

GENTLEMAN

Ay, sir. She took them, read them in my presence,
12 And now and then an ample tear trilled down
Her delicate cheek. It seemed she was a queen
14 Over her passion, who, most rebel-like,
Sought to be king o'er her.

KENT   O, then it movèd her?

GENTLEMAN

Not to a rage. Patience and sorrow strove
17 Who should express her goodliest. You have seen
Sunshine and rain at once – her smiles and tears
19 Were like, a better way: those happy smilets
That played on her ripe lip seemed not to know
What guests were in her eyes, which parted thence
As pearls from diamonds dropped. In brief,
23 Sorrow would be a rarity most belovèd,
If all could so become it.

KENT   Made she no verbal question?

GENTLEMAN

25 Faith, once or twice she heaved the name of father
Pantingly forth, as if it pressed her heart;
Cried 'Sisters, sisters, shame of ladies, sisters!
Kent, father, sisters? What, i' th' storm i' th' night?
29 Let pity not be believed!' There she shook
The holy water from her heavenly eyes,
31 And clamor moistened; then away she started
To deal with grief alone.

KENT   It is the stars,
33 The stars above us govern our conditions;
34 Else one self mate and make could not beget
35 Such different issues. You spoke not with her since?

12 *trilled* trickled   14 *who* which   17 *goodliest* i.e. most becomingly   19
Were . . . way i.e. improved upon that spectacle   23 *rarity* gem   25–26
heaved . . . forth uttered . . . chokingly   29 *Let pity* let it for pity (?)   31
clamor moistened i.e. mixed, and thus muted, lamentation with tears   33
govern our conditions determine our characters   34 *Else . . . make* otherwise
the same husband and wife   35 *issues* children

GENTLEMAN No.

KENT

Was this before the King returned?

GENTLEMAN   No, since.

KENT

Well, sir, the poor distressèd Lear 's i' th' town;
Who sometime, in his better tune, remembers   39
What we are come about, and by no means
Will yield to see his daughter.

GENTLEMAN   Why, good sir?

KENT

A sovereign shame so elbows him; his own unkindness, 42
That stripped her from his benediction, turned her   43
To foreign casualties, gave her dear rights   44
To his dog-hearted daughters – these things sting
His mind so venomously that burning shame
Detains him from Cordelia.

GENTLEMAN   Alack, poor gentleman.

KENT

Of Albany's and Cornwall's powers you heard not?

GENTLEMAN

'Tis so; they are afoot.   49

KENT

Well, sir, I'll bring you to our master Lear
And leave you to attend him. Some dear cause   51
Will in concealment wrap me up awhile.
When I am known aright, you shall not grieve
Lending me this acquaintance. I pray you go
Along with me.   *Exeunt.*]

*

39 *better tune* i.e. more rational state, less jangled   42 *sovereign* overruling;
elbows jogs   43 *stripped* cut off (cf. *disbranch*, IV, ii, 34); *benediction*
blessing   44 *casualties* chances   49 *'Tis so* i.e. I have to this extent   51
dear cause important purpose

IV, iv   *Enter, with Drum and Colors, Cordelia, Gentleman*
           [Doctor], and Soldiers.

CORDELIA
     Alack, 'tis he ! Why, he was met even now
     As mad as the vexed sea, singing aloud,
3   Crowned with rank fumiter and furrow weeds,
4   With hardocks, hemlock, nettles, cuckoo flow'rs,
5   Darnel, and all the idle weeds that grow
6   In our sustaining corn. A century send forth !
     Search every acre in the high-grown field
     And bring him to our eye.   *[Exit an Officer.]*
8   What can man's wisdom
9   In the restoring his bereavèd sense ?
10   He that helps him take all my outward worth.

DOCTOR
     There is means, madam.
12   Our foster nurse of nature is repose,
13   The which he lacks. That to provoke in him
14   Are many simples operative, whose power
     Will close the eye of anguish.

CORDELIA   All blessed secrets,
16   All you unpublished virtues of the earth,
17   Spring with my tears ; be aidant and remediate
     In the good man's distress. Seek, seek for him,
     Lest his ungoverned rage dissolve the life
20   That wants the means to lead it.

           Enter Messenger.

MESSENGER   News, madam.
     The British pow'rs are marching hitherward.

IV, iv A field near Dover   3 *fumiter* fumitory; *furrow weeds* (those that
appear after ploughing?)   4 *hardocks* (variously identified as burdock,
'hoar dock,' 'harlock,' etc.)   5 *Darnel* tares; *idle* useless   6 *sustaining
corn* life-giving wheat; *century* troop of a hundred men   8 *can* i.e. can
accomplish   9 *bereavèd* bereft   10 *outward worth* material possessions
12 *foster* fostering   13 *provoke* induce   14 *simples operative* medicinal
herbs, sedatives   16 *unpublished virtues* i.e. little-known benign herbs
17 *Spring* grow; *remediate* remedial   20 *wants* lacks; *means* i.e. power of
reason; *lead it* govern it (the rage)

CORDELIA
  'Tis known before. Our preparation stands
  In expectation of them. O dear father,
  It is thy business that I go about.
  Therefore great France   25
  My mourning, and importuned tears hath pitied.   26
  No blown ambition doth our arms incite,   27
  But love, dear love, and our aged father's right.
  Soon may I hear and see him!   *Exeunt.*

*

Enter Regan and Steward [Oswald].   IV, v

REGAN
  But are my brother's pow'rs set forth?
OSWALD   Ay, madam.
REGAN
  Himself in person there?
OSWALD   Madam, with much ado.   2
  Your sister is the better soldier.
REGAN
  Lord Edmund spake not with your lord at home?
OSWALD No, madam.
REGAN
  What might import my sister's letter to him?   6
OSWALD I know not, lady.
REGAN
  Faith, he is posted hence on serious matter.   8
  It was great ignorance, Gloucester's eyes being out,   9
  To let him live. Where he arrives he moves
  All hearts against us. Edmund, I think, is gone,
  In pity of his misery, to dispatch

25 *Therefore* therefor, because of that   26 *importuned* importunate   27
blown swollen
IV, v At Gloucester's castle   2 *much ado* great bother   6 *import* bear as
its message   8 *is posted* has sped   9 *ignorance* error

13   His nighted life ; moreover, to descry
       The strength o' th' enemy.

OSWALD

       I must needs after him, madam, with my letter.

REGAN

       Our troops set forth to-morrow. Stay with us.
       The ways are dangerous.

OSWALD   I may not, madam.

18   My lady charged my duty in this business.

REGAN

       Why should she write to Edmund ? Might not you

20   Transport her purposes by word ? Belike,
       Some things – I know not what. I'll love thee much,
       Let me unseal the letter.

OSWALD   Madam, I had rather –

REGAN

       I know your lady does not love her husband,

24   I am sure of that ; and at her late being here

25   She gave strange eliads and most speaking looks

26   To noble Edmund. I know you are of her bosom.

OSWALD I, madam ?

REGAN

       I speak in understanding – y' are, I know't –

29   Therefore I do advise you take this note :
       My lord is dead ; Edmund and I have talked,

31   And more convenient is he for my hand

32   Than for your lady's. You may gather more.

33   If you do find him, pray you give him this ;
       And when your mistress hears thus much from you,

35   I pray desire her call her wisdom to her.
       So fare you well.
       If you do chance to hear of that blind traitor,

---

13 *nighted* benighted, blinded   18 *charged* strictly ordered   20 *Transport her purposes* convey her intentions; *Belike* probably   24 *late* recently   25 *eliads* amorous glances   26 *of her bosom* in her confidence   29 *take this note* note this   31 *convenient* appropriate   32 *gather more* i.e. draw your own conclusions   33 *this* this word, this reminder   35 *call* recall

Preferment falls on him that cuts him off.   38

OSWALD
   Would I could meet him, madam! I should show
   What party I do follow.
REGAN   Fare thee well.   *Exeunt*.

*

Enter Gloucester and Edgar.   IV, vi
GLOUCESTER
   When shall I come to th' top of that same hill?
EDGAR
   You do climb up it now. Look how we labor.
GLOUCESTER
   Methinks the ground is even.
EDGAR   Horrible steep.
   Hark, do you hear the sea?
GLOUCESTER   No, truly.
EDGAR
   Why, then, your other senses grow imperfect
   By your eyes' anguish.   6
GLOUCESTER   So may it be indeed.
   Methinks thy voice is altered, and thou speak'st
   In better phrase and matter than thou didst.
EDGAR
   Y' are much deceived. In nothing am I changed
   But in my garments.
GLOUCESTER   Methinks y' are better spoken.
EDGAR
   Come on, sir; here's the place. Stand still. How fearful
   And dizzy 'tis to cast one's eyes so low!
   The crows and choughs that wing the midway air   13
   Show scarce so gross as beetles. Halfway down   14

38 *Preferment* advancement
IV, vi An open place near Dover   6 *anguish* affliction   13 *choughs* jack-
daws; *midway* i.e. halfway down   14 *gross* large

131

15   Hangs one that gathers sampire – dreadful trade ;
      Methinks he seems no bigger than his head.
      The fishermen that walk upon the beach
18   Appear like mice ; and yond tall anchoring bark,
19   Diminished to her cock ; her cock, a buoy
      Almost too small for sight. The murmuring surge
21   That on th' unnumb'red idle pebble chafes
      Cannot be heard so high. I'll look no more,
23   Lest my brain turn, and the deficient sight
24   Topple down headlong.
      GLOUCESTER   Set me where you stand.
      EDGAR
      Give me your hand. You are now within a foot
      Of th' extreme verge. For all beneath the moon
27   Would I not leap upright.
      GLOUCESTER   Let go my hand.
      Here, friend, 's another purse ; in it a jewel
29   Well worth a poor man's taking. Fairies and gods
      Prosper it with thee. Go thou further off ;
      Bid me farewell, and let me hear thee going.
      EDGAR
      Now fare ye well, good sir.
      GLOUCESTER   With all my heart.
      EDGAR [aside]
33   Why I do trifle thus with his despair
      Is done to cure it.
      GLOUCESTER   O you mighty gods !
             [He kneels.]
      This world I do renounce, and in your sights
      Shake patiently my great affliction off.
37   If I could bear it longer and not fall

15 *sampire* samphire (aromatic herb used in relishes) 18 *anchoring* anchored 19 *Diminished . . . cock* reduced to the size of her cockboat 21 *unnumb'red idle pebble* i.e. barren reach of countless pebbles 23 *the deficient sight* i.e. my dizziness 24 *Topple* topple me 27 *upright* i.e. even upright, let alone forward 29 *Fairies* (the usual wardens of treasure) 33 *Why . . . trifle* i.e. the reason I toy with (*done* in l. 34 being redundant) 37–38 *fall . . . with* i.e. rebel against (irreligiously)

To quarrel with your great opposeless wills,   38
My snuff and loathèd part of nature should   39
Burn itself out. If Edgar live, O bless him!
Now, fellow, fare thee well.
          [He falls forward and swoons.]
EDGAR   Gone, sir – farewell.
And yet I know not how conceit may rob   42
The treasury of life when life itself
Yields to the theft. Had he been where he thought,   44
By this had thought been past. Alive or dead?
Ho you, sir! Friend! Hear you, sir? Speak!
Thus might he pass indeed. Yet he revives.
What are you, sir?
GLOUCESTER   Away, and let me die.
EDGAR
Hadst thou been aught but gossamer, feathers, air,
So many fathom down precipitating,   50
Thou'dst shivered like an egg; but thou dost breathe,
Hast heavy substance, bleed'st not, speak'st, art sound.
Ten masts at each make not the altitude   53
Which thou hast perpendicularly fell.
Thy life's a miracle. Speak yet again.   55
GLOUCESTER
But have I fall'n, or no?
EDGAR
From the dread summit of this chalky bourn.   57
Look up a-height. The shrill-gorged lark so far   58
Cannot be seen or heard. Do but look up.
GLOUCESTER
Alack, I have no eyes.
Is wretchedness deprived that benefit
To end itself by death? 'Twas yet some comfort

---

38 *opposeless* not to be opposed   **39** *My snuff . . . nature* i.e. the guttering
and hateful tag end of my life   **42** *conceit* imagination   **44** *Yields to*
i.e. welcomes   **50** *precipitating* falling   **53** *at each* end to end   **55** *life*
survival   **57** *bourn* boundary, headland   **58** *a-height* on high; *gorged*
throated

63   When misery could beguile the tyrant's rage
        And frustrate his proud will.
    EDGAR   Give me your arm.
65   Up – so. How is't ? Feel you your legs ? You stand.
    GLOUCESTER
        Too well, too well.
    EDGAR   This is above all strangeness.
        Upon the crown o' th' cliff what thing was that
        Which parted from you ?
    GLOUCESTER   A poor unfortunate beggar.
    EDGAR
        As I stood here below, methought his eyes
        Were two full moons ; he had a thousand noses,
71   Horns whelked and waved like the enridgèd sea.
72   It was some fiend. Therefore, thou happy father,
73   Think that the clearest gods, who make them honors
        Of men's impossibilities, have preservèd thee.
    GLOUCESTER
        I do remember now. Henceforth I'll bear
        Affliction till it do cry out itself
        'Enough, enough, and die.' That thing you speak of,
        I took it for a man. Often 'twould say
        'The fiend, the fiend' – he led me to that place.
    EDGAR
80   Bear free and patient thoughts.
                Enter Lear [mad, bedecked with weeds].
                              But who comes here ?
81   The safer sense will ne'er accommodate
82   His master thus.
83 LEAR No, they cannot touch me for coining ; I am the
        King himself.

63 *beguile* outwit 65 *Feel* test 71 *whelked* corrugated; *enridgèd* blown
into ridges 72 *happy father* lucky old man 73 *clearest* purest 73–74
who . . . impossibilities i.e. whose glory it is to do for man what he cannot do
for himself 80 *free* (of despair) 81 *safer* saner; *accommodate* accoutre
82 *His* its 83 *touch* i.e. interfere with; *coining* minting coins (a royal
prerogative)

EDGAR

O thou side-piercing sight!

LEAR Nature 's above art in that respect. There's your 86
press money. That fellow handles his bow like a crow- 87
keeper. Draw me a clothier's yard. Look, look, a mouse! 88
Peace, peace; this piece of toasted cheese will do't.
There's my gauntlet; I'll prove it on a giant. Bring up 90
the brown bills. O, well flown, bird. I' th' clout, i' th' 91
clout – hewgh! Give the word. 92

EDGAR Sweet marjoram. 93

LEAR Pass.

GLOUCESTER

I know that voice.

LEAR Ha! Goneril with a white beard? They flattered me
like a dog, and told me I had the white hairs in my beard 97
ere the black ones were there. To say 'ay' and 'no' to 98
everything that I said! 'Ay' and 'no' too was no good 99
divinity. When the rain came to wet me once, and the
wind to make me chatter; when the thunder would not
peace at my bidding; there I found 'em, there I smelt
'em out. Go to, they are not men o' their words. They
told me I was everything. 'Tis a lie – I am not ague-proof. 104

GLOUCESTER

The trick of that voice I do well remember. 105

---

86 *Nature . . . respect* i.e. a born king is above a made king in legal immunity (cf. the coeval debate on the relative merits of poets of nature, i.e.
born, and poets of art, i.e. made by self-effort)   87 *press money* i.e. the
'king's shilling' (token payment on military impressment or enlistment)
87–88 *crow-keeper* i.e. farmhand warding off crows   88 *clothier's yard* i.e.
arrow (normally a yard long)   90 *gauntlet* armored glove (hurled as challenge); *prove it on* maintain it against   91 *brown bills* varnished halberds;
well flown (hawking cry); *clout* bull's-eye (archery term)   92 *word* pass-
word   93 *Sweet marjoram* (herb, associated with treating madness?)   97
like a dog i.e. fawningly; *I . . . beard* i.e. I was wise   98 *To say . . . 'no'* i.e. to
agree   99–100 *no good divinity* i.e. bad theology (For 'good divinity' cf. 2
Corinthians i, 18: 'But as God is true, our word to you was not yea and nay';
also Matthew v, 36–37, James v, 12.)   104 *ague-proof* proof against chills
and fever   105 *trick* peculiarity

Is't not the King?

LEAR   Ay, every inch a king.
When I do stare, see how the subject quakes.
108   I pardon that man's life. What was thy cause?
Adultery?
Thou shalt not die. Die for adultery? No.
The wren goes to't, and the small gilded fly
112   Does lecher in my sight.
Let copulation thrive; for Gloucester's bastard son
Was kinder to his father than my daughters
115   Got 'tween the lawful sheets.
116   To't, luxury, pell-mell, for I lack soldiers.
Behold yond simp'ring dame,
118   Whose face between her forks presages snow,
119   That minces virtue, and does shake the head
120   To hear of pleasure's name.
121   The fitchew nor the soilèd horse goes to't
With a more riotous appetite.
123   Down from the waist they are Centaurs,
Though women all above.
125   But to the girdle do the gods inherit,
Beneath is all the fiend's.
There's hell, there's darkness, there is the sulphurous
pit; burning, scalding, stench, consumption. Fie, fie,
129   fie! pah, pah! Give me an ounce of civet; good apothe-
cary, sweeten my imagination! There's money for thee.

GLOUCESTER
O, let me kiss that hand.
132 LEAR Let me wipe it first; it smells of mortality.

---

108 *cause* case   **112** *lecher* copulate   **115** *Got* begotten   **116** *luxury* lechery; *for . . . soldiers* (and therefore a higher birth rate)   **118** *Whose . . . snow* i.e. whose face (mien) presages snow (frigidity) between her forks (legs)   **119** *minces* mincingly affects   **120** *pleasure's name* i.e. the very name of sexual indulgence   **121** *fitchew* polecat, prostitute; *soilèd* pastured   **123** *Centaurs* (lustful creatures of mythology, half-human and half-beast)   **125** *girdle* waist; *inherit* possess   **129** *civet* musk perfume   **132** *mortality* death

GLOUCESTER

O ruined piece of nature ; this great world 133
Shall so wear out to naught. Dost thou know me ?

LEAR I remember thine eyes well enough. Dost thou
squiny at me ? No, do thy worst, blind Cupid ; I'll not 136
love. Read thou this challenge ; mark but the penning of it.

GLOUCESTER

Were all thy letters suns, I could not see.

EDGAR [aside]

I would not take this from report – it is, 139
And my heart breaks at it.

LEAR Read.

GLOUCESTER

What, with the case of eyes ? 142

LEAR O, ho, are you there with me ? No eyes in your head, 143
nor no money in your purse ? Your eyes are in a heavy
case, your purse in a light ; yet you see how this world 145
goes.

GLOUCESTER

I see it feelingly. 147

LEAR What, art mad ? A man may see how this world goes
with no eyes. Look with thine ears. See how yond justice
rails upon yond simple thief. Hark in thine ear : change 150
places and, handy-dandy, which is the justice, which is 151
the thief ? Thou hast seen a farmer's dog bark at a beggar ?

GLOUCESTER Ay, sir.

LEAR And the creature run from the cur. There thou
mightst behold the great image of authority – a dog 's 155
obeyed in office.

Thou rascal beadle, hold thy bloody hand ! 157

133-34 *this . . . naught* i.e. the universe (macrocosm) will decay like this
man (microcosm) (cf. III, i, 10n.)   136 *squiny* squint   139 *take* accept
142 *case* sockets   143 *are . . . me* is that the situation   145 *case* plight (pun)
147 *feelingly* (1) only by touch, (2) by feeling pain   150 *simple* mere   151
handy-dandy (old formula used in the child's game of choosing which
hand)   155 *great image* universal symbol   155-56 *a dog's . . . office* i.e.
man bows to authority regardless of who exercises it   157 *beadle* parish
constable

Why dost thou lash that whore? Strip thy own back.

159   Thou hotly lusts to use her in that kind

160   For which thou whip'st her. The usurer hangs the
        cozener.

161   Through tattered clothes small vices do appear;

        Robes and furred gowns hide all. Plate sin with gold,

163   And the strong lance of justice hurtless breaks;

164   Arm it in rags, a pygmy's straw does pierce it.

165   None does offend, none – I say none! I'll able 'em.

166   Take that of me, my friend, who have the power

        To seal th' accuser's lips. Get thee glass eyes

168   And, like a scurvy politician, seem

        To see the things thou dost not. Now, now, now, now!

        Pull off my boots. Harder, harder! So.

EDGAR

171   O, matter and impertinency mixed;

        Reason in madness.

LEAR

If thou wilt weep my fortunes, take my eyes.

I know thee well enough; thy name is Gloucester.

Thou must be patient. We came crying hither;

Thou know'st, the first time that we smell the air

We wawl and cry. I will preach to thee. Mark.

GLOUCESTER

Alack, alack the day.

LEAR

When we are born, we cry that we are come

180   To this great stage of fools. – This' a good block.

181   It were a delicate stratagem to shoe

182   A troop of horse with felt. I'll put't in proof,

---

159 *lusts* wish (suggestive form of 'lists'); *kind* i.e. same act   160 *The usurer . . . cozener* i.e. the great cheat, some moneylending judge, sentences to death the little cheat   161 *appear* show plainly   163 *hurtless* without hurting   164 *Arm . . . rags* i.e. armored (cf. *Plate*, l. 162) only in rags   165 *able* authorize   166 *that* (i.e. the assurance of immunity)   168 *scurvy politician* vile opportunist   171 *matter and impertinency* sense and nonsense   180 *block* felt hat (?)   181 *delicate* subtle   182 *in proof* to the test

And when I have stol'n upon these son-in-laws,
Then kill, kill, kill, kill, kill, kill!
        Enter a Gentleman [with Attendants].

GENTLEMAN
    O, here he is! Lay hand upon him. – Sir,
    Your most dear daughter –

LEAR
    No rescue? What, a prisoner? I am even
    The natural fool of fortune. Use me well;   188
    You shall have ransom. Let me have surgeons;
    I am cut to th' brains.   190

GENTLEMAN   You shall have anything.

LEAR
    No seconds? All myself?
    Why, this would make a man a man of salt,   192
    To use his eyes for garden waterpots,
    [Ay, and laying autumn's dust.] I will die bravely,
    Like a smug bridegroom. What, I will be jovial!   195
    Come, come, I am a king; masters, know you that?

GENTLEMAN
    You are a royal one, and we obey you.

LEAR Then there's life in't. Come, an you get it, you shall   198
    get it by running. Sa, sa, sa, sa!   199
                Exit [running, followed by Attendants].

GENTLEMAN
    A sight most pitiful in the meanest wretch,
    Past speaking of in a king. Thou hast one daughter
    Who redeems Nature from the general curse   202
    Which twain have brought her to.   203

EDGAR
    Hail, gentle sir.

---

188 *natural fool* born plaything   **190** *cut* wounded   **192** *salt* i.e. all tears
195 *smug bridegroom* spruce bridegroom (the image suggested by the
secondary meaning of *bravely*, i.e. handsomely, and the sexual suggestion
of *will die*)   **198** *life* (and therefore 'hope')   **199** *Sa . . . sa* (hunting and
rallying cry)   **202** *general curse* universal condemnation   **203** *twain* i.e.
the other two

204 GENTLEMAN   Sir, speed you. What's your will?

EDGAR

205   Do you hear aught, sir, of a battle toward?

GENTLEMAN

206   Most sure and vulgar. Every one hears that
       Which can distinguish sound.

EDGAR   But, by your favor,
       How near's the other army?

GENTLEMAN

209   Near and on speedy foot. The main descry
       Stands on the hourly thought.

EDGAR   I thank you, sir. That's all

GENTLEMAN
       Though that the Queen on special cause is here,
       Her army is moved on.

EDGAR   I thank you, sir. *Exit [Gentleman].*

GLOUCESTER
       You ever-gentle gods, take my breath from me;

214   Let not my worser spirit tempt me again
       To die before you please.

EDGAR   Well pray you, father.

GLOUCESTER
       Now, good sir, what are you?

EDGAR

217   A most poor man, made tame to fortune's blows,

218   Who, by the art of known and feeling sorrows,

219   Am pregnant to good pity. Give me your hand;

220   I'll lead you to some biding.

GLOUCESTER   Hearty thanks.

221   The bounty and the benison of heaven
       To boot, and boot.

---

204 *speed* God speed   205 *toward* impending   206 *sure and vulgar* commonly known certainty   209 *on speedy foot* rapidly marching   209–10 *main . . . thought* sight of the main body is expected hourly   214 *worser spirit* i.e. bad angel   217 *tame* submissive   218 *art . . . sorrows* i.e. lesson of sorrows painfully experienced   219 *pregnant* prone   220 *biding* biding place   221 *benison* blessing

Enter Steward [Oswald].

OSWALD   A proclaimed prize! Most happy;   222
  That eyeless head of thine was first framed flesh   223
  To raise my fortunes. Thou old unhappy traitor,
  Briefly thyself remember. The sword is out   225
  That must destroy thee.

GLOUCESTER   Now let thy friendly hand   226
  Put strength enough to't.
    [Edgar interposes.]

OSWALD   Wherefore, bold peasant,
  Dar'st thou support a published traitor? Hence,   228
  Lest that th' infection of his fortune take
  Like hold on thee. Let go his arm.

EDGAR
  Chill not let go, zir, without vurther 'casion.   231

OSWALD
  Let go, slave, or thou diest.

EDGAR Good gentleman, go your gait, and let poor voke   233
  pass. An chud ha' bin zwaggered out of my life, 'twould   234
  not ha' bin zo long as 'tis by a vortnight. Nay, come not
  near th' old man. Keep out, che vore ye, or Ise try   236
  whether your costard or my ballow be the harder. Chill   237
  be plain with you.

OSWALD Out, dunghill!
    [They fight.]

EDGAR Chill pick your teeth, zir. Come. No matter vor   240
  your foins.   241
    [Oswald falls.]

OSWALD
  Slave, thou hast slain me. Villain, take my purse.   242

---

222 *proclaimed prize* i.e. one with a price on his head; *happy* lucky   **223**
framed flesh born, created   **225** *thyself remember* i.e. pray, think of your soul
226 *friendly* i.e. unconsciously befriending   **228** *published* proclaimed   **231**
Chill I'll (rustic dialect); *vurther 'casion* further occasion   **233** *gait* way;
voke folk   **234** *An chud* if I could; *zwaggered* swaggered, bluffed   **236** *che*
vore I warrant, assure; *Ise* I shall   **237** *costard* head; *ballow* cudgel   **240**
Chill pick i.e. I'll knock out   **241** *foins* thrusts   **242** *Villain* serf

If ever thou wilt thrive, bury my body,
244 And give the letters which thou find'st about me
To Edmund Earl of Gloucester. Seek him out
246 Upon the English party. O, untimely death!
Death!
[He dies.]

EDGAR
248 I know thee well. A serviceable villain,
249 As duteous to the vices of thy mistress
As badness would desire.

GLOUCESTER   What, is he dead?

EDGAR
Sit you down, father; rest you.
Let's see these pockets; the letters that he speaks of
May be my friends. He's dead; I am only sorry
254 He had no other deathsman. Let us see.
255 Leave, gentle wax and manners: blame us not
256 To know our enemies' minds. We rip their hearts;
257 Their papers is more lawful.
Reads the letter.

'Let our reciprocal vows be remembered. You have
259 many opportunities to cut him off. If your will want not,
time and place will be fruitfully offered. There is nothing done, if he return the conqueror. Then am I the
262 prisoner, and his bed my gaol; from the loathed warmth
whereof deliver me, and supply the place for your labor.
264   'Your (wife, so I would say) affectionate servant,
'Goneril.'

266 O indistinguished space of woman's will—
A plot upon her virtuous husband's life,
268 And the exchange my brother! Here in the sands

---

244 *letters* letter; *about* upon   246 *party* side   248 *serviceable* usable   249 *duteous* ready to serve   254 *deathsman* executioner   255 *Leave, gentle wax* by your leave, kind seal (formula used in opening sealed documents)   256 *To know* i.e. for growing intimate with   257 *Their papers* i.e. to rip their papers   259 *want not* is not lacking   262 *gaol* jail   264 *would* wish to   266 *indistinguished* unlimited; *will* desire   268 *exchange* substitute

Thee I'll rake up, the post unsanctified   269
Of murderous lechers; and in the mature time   270
With this ungracious paper strike the sight   271
Of the death-practiced Duke. For him 'tis well   272
That of thy death and business I can tell.

GLOUCESTER

The King is mad. How stiff is my vile sense,   274
That I stand up, and have ingenious feeling   275
Of my huge sorrows! Better I were distract;   276
So should my thoughts be severed from my griefs,
And woes by wrong imaginations lose   278
The knowledge of themselves.
     Drum afar off.

EDGAR   Give me your hand.
Far off methinks I hear the beaten drum.
Come, father, I'll bestow you with a friend.   *Exeunt.* 281

* * *

     Enter Cordelia, Kent, [Doctor,] and Gentleman.   IV, vii

CORDELIA

O thou good Kent, how shall I live and work
To match thy goodness? My life will be too short
And every measure fail me.

KENT

To be acknowledged, madam, is o'erpaid.
All my reports go with the modest truth;   5
Nor more nor clipped, but so.   6

CORDELIA   Be better suited.
These weeds are memories of those worser hours.   7
I prithee put them off.

---

269 *rake up* cover, bury   270 *in the mature* at the ripe   271 *strike* blast
272 *death-practiced* whose death is plotted   274 *stiff* obstinate; *vile sense*
i.e. hateful consciousness   275 *ingenious feeling* i.e. awareness   276
distract distracted   278 *wrong imaginations* i.e. delusions   281 *bestow*
lodge
IV, vii The French camp near Dover   5 *go* conform   6 *clipped* i.e. less
(curtailed); *suited* attired   7 *weeds* clothes; *memories* reminders

KENT   Pardon, dear madam.
9   Yet to be known shortens my made intent.
10   My boon I make it that you know me not
11   Till time and I think meet.

CORDELIA
   Then be't so, my good lord.
      [To the Doctor]   How does the King?

DOCTOR
   Madam, sleeps still.

CORDELIA
   O you kind gods,
15   Cure this great breach in his abusèd nature!
16   Th' untuned and jarring senses, O, wind up
17   Of this child-changèd father!

DOCTOR   So please your Majesty
   That we may wake the King? He hath slept long.

CORDELIA
   Be governed by your knowledge, and proceed
20   I' th' sway of your own will. Is he arrayed?
     Enter Lear in a chair carried by Servants.

GENTLEMAN
   Ay, madam. In the heaviness of sleep
   We put fresh garments on him.

DOCTOR
   Be by, good madam, when we do awake him.
   I doubt not of his temperance.

[CORDELIA   Very well.
    [Music.]

DOCTOR
   Please you draw near. Louder the music there.]

---

9 *Yet . . . intent* i.e. to reveal myself just yet would mar my plan   10 *My boon
. . . it* the reward I ask is   11 *meet* proper   15 *abusèd* confused, disturbed
16 *jarring* discordant; *wind up* tune   17 *child-changèd* (1) changed to a
child, (2) changed by his children (suggesting 'changeling,' wherein
mental defect is associated with the malignance of witches)   20 *I' th'
sway of* according to

CORDELIA
  O my dear father, restoration hang
  Thy medicine on my lips, and let this kiss
  Repair those violent harms that my two sisters   28
  Have in thy reverence made.   29
KENT   Kind and dear princess.
CORDELIA
  Had you not been their father, these white flakes   30
  Did challenge pity of them. Was this a face   31
  To be opposed against the jarring winds?
  [To stand against the deep dread-bolted thunder?   33
  In the most terrible and nimble stroke
  Of quick cross lightning to watch, poor perdu,   35
  With this thin helm?] Mine enemy's dog,   36
  Though he had bit me, should have stood that night
  Against my fire; and wast thou fain, poor father,   38
  To hovel thee with swine and rogues forlorn
  In short and musty straw? Alack, alack,   40
  'Tis wonder that thy life and wits at once
  Had not concluded all. – He wakes. Speak to him.
DOCTOR
  Madam, do you; 'tis fittest.
CORDELIA
  How does my royal lord? How fares your Majesty?
LEAR
  You do me wrong to take me out o' th' grave.
  Thou art a soul in bliss; but I am bound
  Upon a wheel of fire, that mine own tears   47
  Do scald like molten lead.
CORDELIA   Sir, do you know me?

---

28 *harms* wounds **29** *reverence* reverend person **30** *flakes* strands of hair **31** *challenge* demand **33** *deep dread-bolted* deep-voiced and full of dreadful bolts **35** *perdu* (1) expendable outpost (military term), (2) lost one **36** *helm* military helmet; here, thin hair **38** *fain* glad **40** *short* scanty (?), tramped to fragments (?) **47** *wheel of fire* (implement combining the tortures of breaking and burning, figuring in medieval visions of hell)

LEAR
You are a spirit, I know. Where did you die?

CORDELIA
50   Still, still, far wide!

DOCTOR
He's scarce awake. Let him alone awhile.

LEAR
Where have I been? Where am I? Fair daylight?
53   I am mightily abused. I should e'en die with pity
To see another thus. I know not what to say.
I will not swear these are my hands. Let's see—
I feel this pin prick. Would I were assured
Of my condition.

CORDELIA   O look upon me, sir,
And hold your hand in benediction o'er me.
You must not kneel.

LEAR   Pray, do not mock me.
60   I am a very foolish fond old man,
Fourscore and upward, not an hour more nor less;
And, to deal plainly,
I fear I am not in my perfect mind.
Methinks I should know you, and know this man;
Yet I am doubtful, for I am mainly ignorant
What place this is; and all the skill I have
Remembers not these garments; nor I know not
Where I did lodge last night. Do not laugh at me;
For, as I am a man, I think this lady
To be my child Cordelia.

70 CORDELIA   And so I am! I am!

LEAR
Be your tears wet? Yes, faith. I pray weep not.
If you have poison for me, I will drink it.
I know you do not love me; for your sisters
Have (as I do remember) done me wrong.
You have some cause, they have not.

---

50 *wide* off the mark   **53** *abused* confused

CORDELIA   No cause, no cause.
LEAR
  Am I in France?
KENT   In your own kingdom, sir.
LEAR
  Do not abuse me.   77
DOCTOR
  Be comforted, good madam. The great rage
  You see is killed in him; [and yet it is danger
  To make him even o'er the time he has lost.]   80
  Desire him to go in. Trouble him no more
  Till further settling.   82
CORDELIA
  Will't please your Highness walk?
LEAR   You must bear with me.
  Pray you now, forget and forgive. I am old and foolish.
                      Exeunt. [Manent Kent and Gentleman.]
[GENTLEMAN Holds it true, sir, that the Duke of Corn-
  wall was so slain?
KENT Most certain, sir.
GENTLEMAN Who is conductor of his people?
KENT As 'tis said, the bastard son of Gloucester.
GENTLEMAN They say Edgar, his banished son, is with
  the Earl of Kent in Germany.
KENT Report is changeable. 'Tis time to look about; the
  powers of the kingdom approach apace.   93
GENTLEMAN The arbitrement is like to be bloody. Fare   94
  you well, sir.   *[Exit.]*
KENT
  My point and period will be throughly wrought,   96
  Or well or ill, as this day's battle's fought.   *Exit.]*   97

                              *

77 *abuse* deceive 80 *even o'er* fill in 82 *settling* calming 93 *powers*
armies 94 *arbitrement* decisive action 96 *My point . . . wrought* i.e. my
destiny will be completely worked out 97 *Or* either

                              147

V, i   *Enter, with Drum and Colors, Edmund, Regan,*
         Gentleman, and Soldiers.

EDMUND

1   Know of the Duke if his last purpose hold,
2   Or whether since he is advised by aught
     To change the course. He's full of alteration
4   And self-reproving. Bring his constant pleasure.

                              [Exit an Officer.]

REGAN

5   Our sister's man is certainly miscarried.

EDMUND

6   'Tis to be doubted, madam.

REGAN   Now, sweet lord,

7   You know the goodness I intend upon you.
     Tell me, but truly – but then speak the truth –
     Do you not love my sister?

9 EDMUND   In honored love.

REGAN

     But have you never found my brother's way
11   To the forfended place?

[EDMUND   That thought abuses you.

REGAN

12   I am doubtful that you have been conjunct
     And bosomed with her, as far as we call hers.]

EDMUND

     No, by mine honor, madam.

REGAN

     I never shall endure her. Dear my lord,
     Be not familiar with her.

EDMUND   Fear me not.
     She and the Duke her husband!

V, i An open place near the British camp   **s.d.** *Drum and Colors* drummer
and standard-bearers   1 *Know* learn; *last purpose hold* most recent intention
(i.e. to fight) holds good   2 *advised* induced   4 *constant pleasure* firm
decision   5 *miscarried* met with mishap   6 *doubted* feared   7 *goodness I
intend* boon I plan to confer   9 *honored* honorable   11 *forfended* forbidden; *abuses* deceives   12–13 *doubtful . . . hers* i.e. fearful you have been
intimately linked with her both in mind and body

Enter, with Drum and Colors, Albany, Goneril,
   Soldiers.

[GONERIL *[aside]*
   I had rather lose the battle than that sister
   Should loosen him and me.]   19

ALBANY
   Our very loving sister, well bemet.   20
   Sir, this I heard : the King is come to his daughter,
   With others whom the rigor of our state   22
   Forced to cry out. [Where I could not be honest,   23
   I never yet was valiant. For this business,
   It touches us as France invades our land,   25
   Not bolds the King with others, whom I fear   26
   Most just and heavy causes make oppose.

EDMUND
   Sir, you speak nobly.]

REGAN   Why is this reasoned?   28

GONERIL
   Combine together 'gainst the enemy;
   For these domestic and particular broils   30
   Are not the question here.   31

ALBANY   Let's then determine
   With th' ancient of war on our proceeding.   32

[EDMUND
   I shall attend you presently at your tent.]   33

REGAN
   Sister, you'll go with us?

GONERIL No.

REGAN
   'Tis most convenient. Pray go with us.   36

---

19 *loosen* separate   **20** *bemet* met   **22** *rigor* tyranny   **13** *honest* honorable
25 *touches us as* concerns me because   **26–27** *Not bolds . . . oppose* i.e. but
not because he supports the King and others whose truly great grievances
arouse them to arms   **28** *reasoned* argued   **30** *particular broils* private
quarrels   **31** *question* issue   **32** *th' ancient of war* i.e. seasoned officers
33 *presently* immediately   **36** *convenient* fitting; *with us* (i.e. with her rather
than Edmund as each leads an 'army' from the stage)

GONERIL

37 O ho, I know the riddle. – I will go.

Exeunt both the Armies.

Enter Edgar.

EDGAR *[to Albany]*

38 If e'er your Grace had speech with man so poor,
Hear me one word.

ALBANY *[to those departing]*

I'll overtake you. *[to Edgar]* Speak.

EDGAR

Before you fight the battle, ope this letter.

41 If you have victory, let the trumpet sound
For him that brought it. Wretched though I seem,

43 I can produce a champion that will prove

44 What is avouchèd there. If you miscarry,
Your business of the world hath so an end,

46 And machination ceases. Fortune love you.

ALBANY

Stay till I have read the letter.

EDGAR   I was forbid it.
When time shall serve, let but the herald cry,
And I'll appear again.

ALBANY

50 Why, fare thee well. I will o'erlook thy paper.

Exit [Edgar].

Enter Edmund.

EDMUND

51 The enemy's in view ; draw up your powers.

52 Here is the guess of their true strength and forces

53 By diligent discovery ; but your haste
Is now urged on you.

54 ALBANY   We will greet the time.   *Exit.*

---

37 *riddle* (i.e. the reason for Regan's strange demand)   38 *had speech* i.e.
has condescended to speak   41 *sound* sound a summons   43 *prove* (in
trial by combat)   44 *avouchèd* charged   46 *machination* i.e. all plots and
counterplots   50 *o'erlook* look over   51 *powers* troops   52 *guess* estimate
53 *discovery* reconnoitering   54 *greet* i.e. meet the demands of

EDMUND

  To both these sisters have I sworn my love;
  Each jealous of the other, as the stung   56
  Are of the adder. Which of them shall I take?
  Both? One? Or neither? Neither can be enjoyed,
  If both remain alive. To take the widow
  Exasperates, makes mad her sister Goneril;
  And hardly shall I carry out my side,   61
  Her husband being alive. Now then, we'll use
  His countenance for the battle, which being done,   63
  Let her who would be rid of him devise
  His speedy taking off. As for the mercy
  Which he intends to Lear and to Cordelia –
  The battle done, and they within our power,
  Shall never see his pardon; for my state   68
  Stands on me to defend, not to debate.   *Exit.*

                        *

        Alarum within. Enter, with Drum and Colors, Lear,   V, ii
        [held by the hand by] Cordelia; and Soldiers [of
        France], over the stage and exeunt.
        Enter Edgar and Gloucester.

EDGAR

  Here, father, take the shadow of this tree
  For your good host. Pray that the right may thrive.
  If ever I return to you again,
  I'll bring you comfort.
GLOUCESTER   Grace go with you, sir.   4
                                     Exit [Edgar].
        Alarum and retreat within. Enter Edgar.

---

56 *jealous* suspicious   **61** *hardly . . . side* with difficulty shall I play my part
(as Goneril's lover, or as a great power in England?)   **63** *countenance*
backing   **68–69** *my state . . . debate* i.e. my status depends upon my strength,
not my arguments
V, ii An open place near the field of battle   **4 s.d.** *Alarum and retreat*
(trumpet sounds, signalling the beginning and the ending of a battle)

EDGAR

Away, old man! Give me thy hand. Away!
6   King Lear hath lost, he and his daughter ta'en.
Give me thy hand. Come on.

GLOUCESTER
8   No further, sir. A man may rot even here.

EDGAR
9   What, in ill thoughts again? Men must endure
Their going hence, even as their coming hither;
11   Ripeness is all. Come on.

GLOUCESTER   And that's true too.   *Exeunt.*

V, iii   *Enter, on conquest, with Drum and Colors, Edmund;*
Lear and Cordelia as prisoners; Soldiers, Captain.

EDMUND

Some officers take them away. Good guard
2   Until their greater pleasures first be known
3   That are to censure them.

CORDELIA   We are not the first
4   Who with best meaning have incurred the worst.
For thee, oppressèd king, I am cast down;
Myself could else outfrown false Fortune's frown.
Shall we not see these daughters and these sisters?

LEAR

No, no, no, no! Come, let's away to prison.
We two alone will sing like birds i' th' cage.
10   When thou dost ask me blessing, I'll kneel down
And ask of thee forgiveness. So we'll live,
12   And pray, and sing, and tell old tales, and laugh
At gilded butterflies, and hear poor rogues
Talk of court news; and we'll talk with them too –
Who loses and who wins; who's in, who's out –

6 *ta'en* captured 8 *rot* i.e. die 9 *ill* i.e. suicidal; *endure* put up with, suffer through 11 *Ripeness* i.e. the time decreed by the gods for the fruit to fall from the branch
V, iii 2 *greater pleasures* i.e. the desires of those in higher command 3 *censure* judge 4 *meaning* intentions 10–11 *When . . . forgiveness* (cf. IV, vii, 57–59) 12–14 *laugh . . . news* view with amusement bright ephemera, such as gallants preoccupied with court gossip

And take upon's the mystery of things   16
As if we were God's spies; and we'll wear out,   17
In a walled prison, packs and sects of great ones   18
That ebb and flow by th' moon.

EDMUND   Take them away.

LEAR

Upon such sacrifices, my Cordelia,   20
The gods themselves throw incense. Have I caught thee?
He that parts us shall bring a brand from heaven   22
And fire us hence like foxes. Wipe thine eyes.
The goodyears shall devour them, flesh and fell,   24
Ere they shall make us weep! We'll see 'em starved first.
Come.   *Exeunt [Lear and Cordelia, guarded].*

EDMUND Come hither, captain; hark.
Take thou this note.
         [Gives a paper.] Go follow them to prison.
One step I have advanced thee. If thou dost
As this instructs thee, thou dost make thy way
To noble fortunes. Know thou this, that men
Are as the time is. To be tender-minded   31
Does not become a sword. Thy great employment   32
Will not bear question. Either say thou'lt do't,   33
Or thrive by other means.

CAPTAIN   I'll do't, my lord.

EDMUND

About it; and write happy when th' hast done.   35
Mark, I say instantly, and carry it so
As I have set it down.

16–17 *take . . . spies* i.e. contemplate the wonder of existence as if with divine
insight, seek eternal rather than temporal truths   **17** *wear out* outlast
18–19 *packs . . . moon* i.e. partisan and intriguing clusters of *great ones* who
gain and lose power monthly   **20–21** *Upon . . . incense* i.e. the gods themselves are the celebrants at such sacrificial offerings to love as we are
22–23 *He . . . foxes* i.e. to separate us, as foxes are smoked out and scattered,
would require not a human but a heavenly torch   **24** *goodyears* (un-
defined forces of evil); *fell* hide   **31** *as the time is* (i.e. ruthless in war)
32 *become* befit   **33** *bear question* admit discussion   **35** *write happy*
consider yourself fortunate

[CAPTAIN
    I cannot draw a cart, nor eat dried oats –
    If it be man's work, I'll do't.]   *Exit*
       Flourish. Enter Albany, Goneril, Regan, Soldiers.

ALBANY
    Sir, you have showed to-day your valiant strain,
    And fortune led you well. You have the captives
42 Who were the opposites of this day's strife.
    I do require them of you, so to use them
44 As we shall find their merits and our safety
    May equally determine.

EDMUND   Sir, I thought it fit
    To send the old and miserable King
47 To some retention [and appointed guard];
    Whose age had charms in it, whose title more,
49 To pluck the common bosom on his side
50 And turn our impressed lances in our eyes
    Which do command them. With him I sent the Queen,
    My reason all the same; and they are ready
53 To-morrow, or at further space, t' appear
54 Where you shall hold your session. [At this time
    We sweat and bleed, the friend hath lost his friend,
56 And the best quarrels, in the heat, are cursed
57 By those that feel their sharpness.
    The question of Cordelia and her father
    Requires a fitter place.]

ALBANY   Sir, by your patience,
60 I hold you but a subject of this war,
    Not as a brother.

61 REGAN   That's as we list to grace him.
    Methinks our pleasure might have been demanded
    Ere you had spoke so far. He led our powers,

42 *opposites of* enemies in   44 *merits* deserts   47 *some . . . guard* detention under duly appointed guards   49 *pluck . . . bosom* draw popular sympathy 50 *turn . . . eyes* i.e. make our conscripted lancers turn on us   53 *space* interval   54 *session* trials   56 *best quarrels* worthiest causes   57 *sharpness* i.e. painful effects   60 *subject of* subordinate in   61 *list to grace* please to honor

Bore the commission of my place and person,
The which immediacy may well stand up   65
And call itself your brother.

GONERIL   Not so hot!
In his own grace he doth exalt himself
More than in your addition.   68

REGAN   In my rights
By me invested, he compeers the best.   69

ALBANY
That were the most if he should husband you.   70

REGAN
Jesters do oft prove prophets.

GONERIL   Holla, holla!
That eye that told you so looked but asquint.   72

REGAN
Lady, I am not well; else I should answer
From a full-flowing stomach. General,   74
Take thou my soldiers, prisoners, patrimony;   75
Dispose of them, of me; the walls is thine.   76
Witness the world that I create thee here
My lord and master.

GONERIL   Mean you to enjoy him?

ALBANY
The let-alone lies not in your good will.   79

EDMUND
Nor in thine, lord.

ALBANY   Half-blooded fellow, yes.   80

REGAN [to Edmund]
Let the drum strike, and prove my title thine.   81

ALBANY
Stay yet; hear reason. Edmund, I arrest thee

---

65 *immediacy* i.e. present status (as my deputy)   68 *your addition* honors
conferred by you   69 *compeers* equals   70 *most* i.e. most complete investi-
ture in your rights; *husband* wed   72 *asquint* cross-eyed, crookedly   74
stomach anger   75 *patrimony* inheritance   76 *walls is thine* i.e. you have
stormed the citadel (myself)   79 *let-alone* permission   80 *Half-blooded*
i.e. by birth only half noble   81 *Let . . . thine* i.e. fight and win for yourself
my rights in the kingdom

83 On capital treason ; and, in thy attaint,
This gilded serpent.
          [Points to Goneril.] For your claim, fair sister,
I bar it in the interest of my wife.
86 'Tis she is subcontracted to this lord,
87 And I, her husband, contradict your banes.
88 If you will marry, make your loves to me ;
My lady is bespoke.

89 GONERIL   An interlude !

ALBANY
Thou art armed, Gloucester. Let the trumpet sound.
If none appear to prove upon thy person
Thy heinous, manifest, and many treasons,
There is my pledge.
93   *[Throws down a glove.]* I'll make it on thy heart,
94 Ere I taste bread, thou art in nothing less
Than I have here proclaimed thee.

REGAN   Sick, O sick !

GONERIL *[aside]*
96 If not, I'll ne'er trust medicine.

EDMUND
There's my exchange.
          [Throws down a glove.] What in the world he is
That names me traitor, villain-like he lies.
99 Call by the trumpet. He that dares approach,
On him, on you, who not ? I will maintain
My truth and honor firmly.

ALBANY
A herald, ho !

[EDMUND   A herald, ho, a herald !]

83 *in thy attaint* i.e. as party to your corruption (cf. the *serpent* of Eden)
86 *subcontracted* i.e. engaged, though previously married (sarcastic play on
'precontracted,' a legal term applied to one facing an impediment to
marriage because previously engaged to another) **87** *contradict your banes*
forbid your banns, i.e. declare an impediment **88** *loves* love-suits **89** *An
interlude* a quaint playlet (equivalent to saying 'How dramatic!' or 'How
comical!') **93** *make* prove **94** *nothing less* i.e. no respect less guilty **96**
medicine i.e. poison **99** *trumpet* trumpeter

ALBANY
  Trust to thy single virtue; for thy soldiers,   103
  All levied in my name, have in my name
  Took their discharge.
REGAN   My sickness grows upon me.
ALBANY
  She is not well. Convey her to my tent.
                              [Exit Regan, attended.]
        Enter a Herald.
  Come hither, herald. Let the trumpet sound,
  And read out this.
[CAPTAIN Sound, trumpet!]
        A trumpet sounds.
HERALD *(reads)* 'If any man of quality or degree within 110
  the lists of the army will maintain upon Edmund, sup- 111
  posed Earl of Gloucester, that he is a manifold traitor,
  let him appear by the third sound of the trumpet. He is
  bold in his defense.'
[EDMUND Sound!]
        First trumpet.
HERALD Again!
        Second trumpet.
  Again!
        Third trumpet.
        Trumpet answers within.
        *Enter Edgar, armed [at the third sound, a Trumpeter
        before him].*
ALBANY
  Ask him his purposes, why he appears
  Upon this call o' th' trumpet.
HERALD   What are you?
  Your name, your quality, and why you answer
  This present summons?
EDGAR   Know my name is lost,
  By treason's tooth bare-gnawn and canker-bit;   122

103 *single virtue* unaided prowess 110 *degree* rank 111 *lists* muster
122 *canker-bit* eaten, as by the rose-caterpillar

Yet am I noble as the adversary
I come to cope.

ALBANY   Which is that adversary?

EDGAR
What's he that speaks for Edmund Earl of Gloucester?

EDMUND
Himself. What say'st thou to him?

EDGAR   Draw thy sword.
That, if my speech offend a noble heart,
Thy arm may do thee justice. Here is mine.

129   Behold it is my privilege,
The privilege of mine honors,
My oath, and my profession. I protest—

132   Maugre thy strength, place, youth, and eminence,
133   Despite thy victor sword and fire-new fortune,
134   Thy valor and thy heart—thou art a traitor,
False to thy gods, thy brother, and thy father,
136   Conspirant 'gainst this high illustrious prince,
137   And from th' extremest upward of thy head
138   To the descent and dust below thy foot
139   A most toad-spotted traitor. Say thou 'no,'
140   This sword, this arm, and my best spirits are bent
To prove upon thy heart, whereto I speak,
Thou liest.

142 EDMUND   In wisdom I should ask thy name,
But since thy outside looks so fair and warlike,
144   And that thy tongue some say of breeding breathes,
145   What safe and nicely I might well delay
By rule of knighthood I disdain and spurn.
147   Back do I toss these treasons to thy head,

129–31 *it . . . profession* i.e. wielding this sword is the privilege of my knightly honor, oath, and function 132 *Maugre* in spite of 133 *fire-new* brand-new 134 *heart* courage 136 *Conspirant* in conspiracy 137 *extremest upward* uppermost extreme 138 *descent and dust* i.e. all that intervenes from the head to the dust 139 *toad-spotted* i.e. exuding venom like a toad 140 *bent* directed 142 *wisdom* prudence 144 *some say* some assay, i.e. proof (?), one might say (?) 145 *safe and nicely* cautiously and punctiliously 147 *treasons* accusations of treason

With the hell-hated lie o'erwhelm thy heart,   148
Which – for they yet glance by and scarcely bruise –   149
This sword of mine shall give them instant way
Where they shall rest for ever. Trumpets, speak!
   Alarums. Fight. [Edmund falls.]

ALBANY
Save him, save him.   152

GONERIL   This is practice, Gloucester.
By th' law of war thou wast not bound to answer
An unknown opposite. Thou art not vanquished,
But cozened and beguiled.   155

ALBANY   Shut your mouth, dame,
Or with this paper shall I stop it. – Hold, sir. –   156
   [To Goneril]
Thou worse than any name, read thine own evil.
No tearing, lady! I perceive you know it.

GONERIL
Say if I do – the laws are mine, not thine.   159
 Who can arraign me for't?

ALBANY   Most monstrous! O,
Know'st thou this paper?

GONERIL   Ask me not what I know. *Exit.*

ALBANY
Go after her. She's desperate; govern her.   162
                    [Exit an Officer.]

EDMUND
What you have charged me with, that have I done,
And more, much more. The time will bring it out.
'Tis past, and so am I. – But what art thou
That hast this fortune on me? If thou'rt noble,   166
I do forgive thee.

---

148 *hell-hated* hateful as hell   **149–51** *Which . . . ever* i.e. the accusations of
treason, now flying about harmlessly, will be routed into you with my sword-
thrust and lodge there permanently   **152** *Save him* spare him (cf. l. 156);
practice trickery   **155** *cozened* cheated   **156** *Hold* wait (If addressed to
Edmund, this suggests a motive for the *Save him* of l. 152: i.e. Albany hopes
to obtain a confession.)   **159** *mine* (i.e. as ruler)   **162** *govern* control   **166**
fortune on i.e. victory over

167 EDGAR   Let's exchange charity.
    I am no less in blood than thou art, Edmund;
169 If more, the more th' hast wronged me.
    My name is Edgar and thy father's son.
171 The gods are just, and of our pleasant vices
    Make instruments to plague us.
173 The dark and vicious place where thee he got
    Cost him his eyes.

EDMUND   Th' hast spoken right; 'tis true.
175 The wheel is come full circle; I am here.

ALBANY
176 Methought thy very gait did prophesy
    A royal nobleness. I must embrace thee.
    Let sorrow split my heart if ever I
    Did hate thee, or thy father.

EDGAR   Worthy prince, I know't.

ALBANY
    Where have you hid yourself?
    How have you known the miseries of your father?

EDGAR
    By nursing them, my lord. List a brief tale;
    And when 'tis told, O that my heart would burst!
    The bloody proclamation to escape
185 That followed me so near (O our lives' sweetness,
    That we the pain of death would hourly die
    Rather than die at once!) taught me to shift
    Into a madman's rags, t' assume a semblance
189 That very dogs disdained; and in this habit
190 Met I my father with his bleeding rings,
    Their precious stones new lost; became his guide,
    Led him, begged for him, saved him from despair;

---

167 *charity* forgiveness and love   **169** *If more* if greater (since legitimate)
171 *of our pleasant* out of our pleasurable   **173** *place* i.e. the bed of adultery;
got begot   **175** *wheel* (of fortune); *here* (at its bottom)   **176** *prophesy*
promise   **185–86** *O . . . die* i.e. how sweet is life that we would prefer to
suffer death-pangs hourly   **189** *habit* attire   **190** *rings* sockets

Never – O fault ! – revealed myself unto him
Until some half hour past, when I was armed,   194
Not sure, though hoping of this good success,
I asked his blessing, and from first to last
Told him our pilgrimage. But his flawed heart –   197
Alack, too weak the conflict to support –
'Twixt two extremes of passion, joy and grief,
Burst smilingly.

EDMUND   This speech of yours hath moved me,
And shall perchance do good ; but speak you on –
You look as you had something more to say.

ALBANY
If there be more, more woeful, hold it in,
For I am almost ready to dissolve,   204
Hearing of this.

[EDGAR   This would have seemed a period   205
To such as love not sorrow ; but another,   206
To amplify too much, would make much more,
And top extremity.
Whilst I was big in clamor, came there in a man,   209
Who, having seen me in my worst estate,   210
Shunned my abhorred society ; but then, finding
Who 'twas that so endured, with his strong arms
He fastened on my neck, and bellowed out
As he'd burst heaven, threw him on my father,
Told the most piteous tale of Lear and him
That ever ear received ; which in recounting
His grief grew puissant, and the strings of life   217
Began to crack. Twice then the trumpets sounded,
And there I left him tranced.   219

ALBANY   But who was this ?

---

194 *armed* in armor   **197** *our pilgrimage* of our journey; *flawed* cracked
204 *dissolve* melt into tears   **205** *a period* the limit   **206–08** *another . . .
extremity* i.e. another sorrow, too fully described, would exceed the limit
209 *big in clamor* loud in lamentation   **210** *estate* state   **217** *puissant*
powerful   **219** *tranced* insensible

EDGAR
Kent, sir, the banished Kent; who in disguise
221   Followed his enemy king and did him service
Improper for a slave.]
     Enter a Gentleman [with a bloody knife].

GENTLEMAN
Help, help! O, help!

EDGAR   What kind of help?

ALBANY   Speak, man.

EDGAR
What means this bloody knife?

224   GENTLEMAN   'Tis hot, it smokes.
It came even from the heart of – O, she's dead.

ALBANY
Who dead? Speak, man.

GENTLEMAN
Your lady, sir, your lady; and her sister
By her is poisonèd; she confesses it.

EDMUND
229   I was contracted to them both. All three
230   Now marry in an instant.

EDGAR   Here comes Kent.
     Enter Kent.

ALBANY
Produce the bodies, be they alive or dead.
                    [Exit Gentleman.]
This judgment of the heavens, that makes us tremble,
Touches us not with pity. – O, is this he?
234   The time will not allow the compliment
235   Which very manners urges.

KENT   I am come
To bid my king and master aye good night.
Is he not here?

---

221 *enemy* inimical 224 *smokes* steams 229 *contracted* engaged 230
marry (i.e. in death) 234 *compliment* ceremony 235 *very manners* i.e.
sheer decency

ALBANY   Great thing of us forgot!   237
  Speak, Edmund, where's the King? and where's
    Cordelia?
        Goneril and Regan's bodies brought out.
  Seest thou this object, Kent?   239

KENT
  Alack, why thus?

EDMUND   Yet Edmund was beloved.   240
  The one the other poisoned for my sake,
  And after slew herself.

ALBANY
  Even so. Cover their faces.

EDMUND
  I pant for life. Some good I mean to do,   244
  Despite of mine own nature. Quickly send –
  Be brief in it – to th' castle, for my writ   246
  Is on the life of Lear and on Cordelia.
  Nay, send in time.

ALBANY   Run, run, O run!

EDGAR
  To who, my lord? Who has the office? Send   249
  Thy token of reprieve.

EDMUND
  Well thought on. Take my sword;
  Give it the captain.

EDGAR   Haste thee for thy life. *[Exit Officer.]*

EDMUND
  He hath commission from thy wife and me
  To hang Cordelia in the prison and
  To lay the blame upon her own despair
  That she fordid herself.   256

ALBANY
  The gods defend her! Bear him hence awhile.
                              [Edmund is borne off.]

---

237 *thing* matter; *of* by   **239** *object* sight   **240** *Yet* despite all   **244** *pant for life* i.e. gasp for life's breath   **246** *writ* i.e. order of execution   **249** *office* commission   **256** *fordid* destroyed

Enter Lear, with Cordelia in his arms [, Gentleman,
and others following].

LEAR

Howl, howl, howl! O, you are men of stones.
Had I your tongues and eyes, I'ld use them so
That heaven's vault should crack. She's gone for ever.
I know when one is dead, and when one lives.
She's dead as earth. Lend me a looking glass.

263 If that her breath will mist or stain the stone,
Why then she lives.

264 KENT   Is this the promised end?

EDGAR

265 Or image of that horror?

ALBANY   Fall and cease.

LEAR

This feather stirs; she lives! If it be so,

267 It is a chance which does redeem all sorrows
That ever I have felt.

KENT   O my good master.

LEAR

Prithee away.

EDGAR   'Tis noble Kent, your friend.

LEAR

A plague upon you murderers, traitors all;
I might have saved her; now she's gone for ever.
Cordelia, Cordelia, stay a little. Ha,
What is't thou say'st? Her voice was ever soft,
Gentle, and low – an excellent thing in woman.
I killed the slave that was a-hanging thee.

GENTLEMAN

'Tis true, my lords, he did.

LEAR   Did I not, fellow?

277 I have seen the day, with my good biting falchion
I would have made them skip. I am old now,

263 *stone* i.e. glass   264 *promised end* i.e. doomsday   265 *image* duplicate;
Fall and cease i.e. strike once and for all, make an end of things   267
redeem atone for   277 *falchion* small sword slightly hooked

And these same crosses spoil me. Who are you? 279
Mine eyes are not o' th' best, I'll tell you straight. 280

KENT

If Fortune brag of two she loved and hated, 281
One of them we behold.

LEAR

This is a dull sight. Are you not Kent? 283

KENT   The same:
Your servant Kent; where is your servant Caius? 284

LEAR

He's a good fellow, I can tell you that.
He'll strike, and quickly too. He's dead and rotten.

KENT

No, my good lord; I am the very man.

LEAR

I'll see that straight. 288

KENT

That from your first of difference and decay 289
Have followed your sad steps.

LEAR   You are welcome hither.

KENT

Nor no man else. All's cheerless, dark, and deadly. 291
Your eldest daughters have fordone themselves, 292
And desperately are dead. 293

LEAR   Ay, so I think.

ALBANY

He knows not what he says; and vain is it
That we present us to him.

EDGAR   Very bootless. 295

---

279 *crosses* adversities; *spoil me* i.e. sap my strength   **280** *tell you straight* admit (?), recognize you in a moment (?)   **281** *two* (i.e. Lear, and a hypothetical second extreme example of Fortune's cruelty with whom he may be equated); *loved and hated* i.e. favored, then victimized   **283** *sight* eyesight (instinctively Lear shuns the admission that he is dazed and weeping)   **284** *Caius* (Kent's alias)   **288** *see that straight* understand that in a moment   **289** *difference and decay* change and decline in fortune   **291** *Nor no man else* i.e. no, nor anyone else   **292** *fordone* destroyed   **293** *desperately* in a state of despair   **295** *bootless* useless

Enter a Messenger.

MESSENGER
Edmund is dead, my lord.

ALBANY   That's but a trifle here.
You lords and noble friends, know our intent.
298 What comfort to this great decay may come
Shall be applied. For us, we will resign,
During the life of this old Majesty,
To him our absolute power ; *[to Edgar and Kent]* you to
   your rights,
302 With boot and such addition as your honors
Have more than merited. All friends shall taste
The wages of their virtue, and all foes
The cup of their deservings. – O, see, see !

LEAR
306 And my poor fool is hanged : no, no, no life ?
Why should a dog, a horse, a rat, have life,
And thou no breath at all ? Thou'lt come no more,
Never, never, never, never, never.
Pray you undo this button. Thank you, sir.
Do you see this ? Look on her ! Look her lips,
Look there, look there –
   He dies.

EDGAR   He faints. My lord, my lord –

KENT
Break, heart, I prithee break !

EDGAR   Look up, my lord.

KENT
314 Vex not his ghost. O, let him pass ! He hates him
315 That would upon the rack of this tough world
Stretch him out longer.

EDGAR   He is gone indeed.

298 *What . . . come* i.e. whatever means of aiding this ruined great one
presents itself   302 *boot* good measure; *addition* titles, advancement in
rank   306 *fool* i.e. Cordelia ('Fool' was often a term of affection, and sometimes, as in Erasmus and elsewhere in Shakespeare, of praise – an ironic
commentary upon self-seeking 'worldly wisdom.')   314 *Vex . . . ghost* do
not trouble his departing spirit   315 *rack* instrument of torture

KENT

The wonder is he hath endured so long;
He but usurped his life.   318

ALBANY

Bear them from hence. Our present business
Is general woe.
        [To Kent and Edgar] Friends of my soul, you twain
Rule in this realm, and the gored state sustain.

KENT

I have a journey, sir, shortly to go.
My master calls me; I must not say no.

EDGAR

The weight of this sad time we must obey,   324
Speak what we feel, not what we ought to say.
The oldest hath borne most; we that are young
Shall never see so much, nor live so long.
                              Exeunt with a dead march.

---

318 *usurped* possessed contrary to (natural) law   324 *obey* i.e. accept

APPENDIX: THE QUARTO TEXT

The present edition, as explained in the "Note on the text," adheres closely to the folio version of the play. The quarto version, although inferior in the main, is of great literary interest. The essential material for a comparison of the verbal features of the two versions is here supplied.

Mechanically, the quarto text is very defective: stage directions are often lacking and the speakers are confusingly designated; the punctuation is bad; and the verse is often printed as prose, the prose as verse. Omitted from the quarto but included in the folio are passages totalling approximately 100 lines, appearing in the present edition at the following points:

I, i, 40–45 *while . . . now*   49–50 *Since . . . state*   64–65 *and . . . rivers*   83–85 *to whose . . . interest*   88–89 *Nothing . . . Nothing*   162 *Dear sir, forbear*

I, ii 107–12 *This villain . . . graves*   160–65 *I pray . . . brother*

I, iv, 252 *Pray . . . patient*   265 *Of . . . you*   313–24 *This man . . . Oswald*

II, iv, 6 *No, my lord*   21 *By Juno . . . ay*   45–53 *Winter's . . . year*   93–94 *Well . . . man*   98 *Are . . . blood*   135–40 *Say . . . blame*   291–92 *Whither . . . horse*

III, i, 22–29 *Who have . . . furnishings*

III, ii, 79–96 *This . . . time*

III, iv, 17–18 *In . . . endure*   26–27 *In, boy . . . sleep*   37–38 *Fathom . . . Tom*

III, vi, 12–14 *No . . . him*   83 *And . . . noon*

IV, i, 6–9 *Welcome . . . blasts*

IV, ii, 25 *My . . . Gloucester*

IV, vi, 162–67 *Plate . . . lips*

V, ii, 11 *And . . . too*

V, iii, 76 *Dispose . . . thine*   89 *An interlude*   145 *What . . . delay*
223 *Speak, man*   311–12 *Do . . . there*

On the other hand, included in the quarto but omitted from the
folio are passages totalling approximately 283 lines – inserted in
square brackets in the present edition at the following points:

I, i, 104   I, ii, 93–95, 140–47   I, iii, 16–20, 24–25   I, iv, 133–48,
222–25, 248, 295   II, i, 78   II, ii, 136–40, 146   II, iv, 18–19
III, i, 7–15, 30–42   III, vi, 17–55, 95–99, 100–13   III, vii, 99–
107   IV, i, 58–63   IV, ii, 31–50, 53–59, 62–68, 69   IV, iii, 1–55
IV, vi, 194   IV, vii, 24–25, 33–36, 79–80, 85–97   V, i, 11–13,
18–19, 23–28, 33   V, iii, 38–39, 47, 54–59, 102, 109, 115, 205–22.

In addition, the following words in the present edition represent
insertions from the quarto: I, i, 214 *best*   289 *not*   I, ii, 127 *Fut*
129 *Edgar*   130 *and*   166 *Go armed*   II, i, 71 *ay*   II, iii, 15 *bare*
III, iv, 127 *had*   IV, vii, 24 *not*   V, i, 16 *me*

The wording of the quarto text differs from that of the folio
in hundreds of instances. In the present edition a quarto reading
has been substituted for a folio reading only when the latter makes
poor or obviously inferior sense. The list of such substitutions
follows, with the adopted quarto readings in italics followed by the
folio readings in roman. (In this appendix the readings of the
quarto as well as the folio are given in modern spelling.)

I, i, 5 *equalities* qualities   74 *possesses* professes   170 *sentence*
sentences   188 *Gloucester* Cordelia   206 *on* in   221 *Fall'n* Fall
225 *well* will   248 *respects of fortune* respect and fortunes   302
hit sit
I, iv, 1 *well* will   93 *Kent. Why, fool* Lear. Why, my boy   163 *e'er*
(from '*euer*') ere   169 *fools* fool   194 *endurèd* endured   334
atasked at task
II, i, 70 *I should* should I   79 *why* where   87 *strange news* strange-
ness   115 *Natures* Nature's
II, ii, 21 *clamorous* clamors   70 *too* t'   73 *Renege* Revenge   74
gale gall   118 *dread* dead   125 *respect* respects
II, iv, 2 *messenger* messengers   30 *panting* painting   33 *whose*
those   126 *mother's* mother   181 *fickle* 'fickly'
III, ii, 3 *drowned* drown

III, iv, 52 *ford* sword   86 *deeply* dearly   109 *till the* at   126 *stock-punished* stocked, punished
III, v, 24 *dearer* dear
III, vi, 68 *tike* tight   75 *makes* make
IV, i, 41 *Then prithee get thee gone* Get thee away
IV, ii, 75 *thereat enraged* threat-enraged   79 *justicers* justices
IV, iv, 18 *distress* desires
IV, vi, 17 *walk* walked   71 *enridgèd* enragèd   83 *coining* crying
161 *small* great   201 *one* a
V, i, 46 *love* loves
V, iii, 83 *attaint* arrest   84 *sister* sisters   97 *he is* he's   161 *Goneril Bastard* (i.e. Edmund)   278 *them* him

Omitted from the above list are a few instances of variation in which a folio misprint would have been detectable without reference to the quarto. Omitted from the following list are numerous instances of slight variation between quarto and folio in the use of articles, prepositions, elision, number, tense, etc., in which the literary interest is small. In all such instances the folio has been followed in the present edition, as well as in the variations listed below. Here the adopted folio readings are in italics followed by the quarto readings in roman. The great majority of the latter are, by common consent, inferior, but while these cast suspicion upon all, the fact remains that a certain number are not inferior to the folio readings and may represent what Shakespeare actually wrote. Marked with stars are the quarto readings which seem to the present editor best able to compete with the folio readings when judged from a purely literary point of view.

I, i, 20 *to* into   34 *the* my   35 *lord* liege   37 *Give me the map there. Know that we have divided* *The map there. Know we have divided   38 *fast* first   39 *from our age* of our state   40 *Conferring* Confirming   *strengths* years   45 *The princes* The two great princes   53 *Where nature doth with merit challenge* Where merit doth most challenge it   55 *love* do love   62 *speak* do   64 *shadowy* shady   68 *of Cornwall* *to Cornwall? Speak   69 *of that self mettle as my sister* of the selfsame mettle that my sister is   72 *comes too* came   78 *ponderous* richer   82 *conferred* confirmed   83 *our last and least* the last, not least in our dear love   85 *draw* win   86 *sisters? Speak* sisters   90 *Nothing will* How? Nothing can   94 *How, how, Cordelia* Go to, Go to   95

you it   108 *Let* Well, let   118 *shall to my bosom* shall   130 *with*
in   135 *shall* still   149 *falls* *stoops   *Reserve thy state* *Reverse
thy doom   156 *ne'er* nor   157 *motive* the motive   161 *Miscreant* Recreant   163 *Kill* Do. Kill   164 *gift* doom   166 *Hear
me, recreant* Hear me   168 *That* Since   *vows* vow   169 *strained*
strayed   173 *Five* Four   174 *disasters* *diseases   175 *sixth*
fifth   180 *Fare* Why, fare   181 *Freedom* Friendship   182 *dear
shelter* protection   190 *this* a   193 *Most royal* Royal   194 *hath*
what   200 *more* else   202 *Will* Sir, will   204 *Dow'red* Covered
214 *whom* that   216 *The best, the dearest* Most best, most
dearest   223 *Should* Could   226 *make known* may know
228 *unchaste* *unclean   230 *richer* rich   232 *That* As   233
Better Go, to, go to. Better   235 *but* no more but   239 *regards*
respects   241 *a dowry* and dower   *King* Lear   258 *of* in   259
Can Shall   271 *Love* Use   276 *duty* duties   280 *plighted*
pleated   281 *with shame* shame them   283 *not little* not a little
291 *grossly* gross   305 *of it* on't

I, ii, 10 *With base? with baseness? Bastardy base? Base* With base,
base bastardy   15 *then* the   18 *legitimate. Fine word, 'legitimate'* legitimate   24 *prescribed* subscribed   38 *o'erlooking*
liking   45 *policy and reverence* policy   68 *before* heretofore   70
heard him oft often heard him   72 *declined* declining   76
sirrah sir   *I'll* I   85 *that he hath writ* he hath wrote   86 *other*
further   100 *find* see   103 *reason it* reason   118 *on* by   120
spherical spiritual   124 *on* to   *a star* stars   129 *bastardizing* bastardy   130 *pat* out   131 *Tom o'* them of   132–33
divisions. Fa, sol, la, mi divisions   138 *with* about   139 *writes*
writ   148 *The night* Why, the night   150 *Ay, two* Two

I, iii, 13 *fellows* fellow servants   *to* in   14 *distaste* dislike   18 *my*
our   21 *have said* tell you   *Well* Very well   26 *course* *very
course   *Prepare* Go prepare

I, iv, 20 *be'st* be   30 *canst thou* canst   43 *You, you* You   68 *my*
this   72 *noted it well* noted it   75 *you, sir, you* you sir, you sir
hither, sir hither   78–79 *your pardon* you pardon me   81 *strucken*
struck   85 *sir, arise, away* sir   87 *Go to! Have you wisdom? So*
You have wisdom   97 *did* done   106 *the Lady Brach* Lady o'
the Brach   111 *nuncle* uncle   122 *Kent* Lear   123 *'tis like* like
125 *nuncle* uncle   131 *sweet one* sweet fool   158 *grace* wit   160
And They   *to wear* do wear   172 *lie, sirrah* lie   181 *You*
*Methinks you   183 *frowning* *frown   188 *nor crust* neither
crust   204 *Will* Must   205 *know* trow   210 *I would* Come,

sir, I would *your* that 212 *transport* transform 216 *This* Why, this 219 *Ha! Waking? 'Tis* Sleeping or waking? Ha! Sure 'tis 227 *This admiration, sir* Come, sir, this admiration 229 *To understand* Understand 236 *graced* great 237 *then* thou 248 *Woe* We *repents* repent's 261 *Lear, Lear, Lear* Lear, Lear 266 *Hear* Hark 280 *Away, away* Go, go, my people 282 *more of it* the cause 294 *loose* make 296 *Ha! Let it be so. I have another daughter* *Let it be so. Yet have I left a daughter 301 *ever* ever. Thou shalt, I warrant thee *that* that, my lord 304 *Pray you, content. – What, Oswald, ho* Come, sir, no more 306 *tarry* tarry and 331 *No, no,* Now 333 *condemn* dislike

I, v, 4 *afore* before 10 *not* ne'er 14 *can tell what* can what 15 *What canst tell, boy* Why, what canst thou tell, my boy 17 *canst* canst not *i' th' middle on's* in the middle of his 31 *moe* more 33 *Yes indeed* Yes 38 *till* before 40 *O, let me not be mad, not mad, sweet heaven* O, let me not be mad, sweet heaven. I would not be mad 42 *How now, are* Are 45 *that's a* that is 46 *unless* except

II, i, 3–4 *Regan his Duchess* his Duchess 4 *this* to 7 *they* there 8 *ear-kissing* *ear-bussing 11 *the* the two 13 *may do* may 18 *I must act. Briefness* must ask briefness *work* help 23 *Cornwall* Cornwall ought 27 *yourself* your – 30 *Draw, seem* Seem 31 *ho* here 32 *Fly, brother* Fly, brother, fly 39 *Mumbling* Warbling 40 *stand* stand's 43 *him, ho* him 46 *the thunder* *their thunders 52 *latched* lanched 56 *Full* But 62 *coward* caitiff 68 *would the reposal* could the reposure 73 *practice* pretence 76 *spirits* *spurs 77 *O strange* *Strong 78 *letter, said he* letter 90 *O madam* Madam *it's cracked* *is cracked 97 *he was of that consort* he was 100 *th' expense and waste* the waste and spoil 120 *prize* poise

II, ii, 1 *dawning* even 5 *lov'st* love 15–16 *action-taking* action-taking knave. A 16 *superserviceable, finical* superfinical 21 *deny'st* deny 28 *night, yet* night 29 *You* Draw, you 32 *come with* bring 39 *Murder, murder* Murder! help 40 *matter?* Part matter 54 *they* he 55 *years o' th' trade* hours at the trade 64 *know you* you have 69 *atwain* in twain 72 *Being* *Bring *the* *their 79 *drive* send 84 *fault* offense 90 *some* a 94 *An honest mind and plain* He must be plain 100 *faith* sooth 101 *great* grand 103 *mean'st* mean'st thou 113 *compact* conjunct 120 *Fetch* Bring 121 *ancient* miscreant 122 *Sir, I* I

127 *Stocking* Stopping   133 *color* nature   141 *King his master needs must* King must   142 *he* he's   147 *Cornwall. Come, my lord, away* *Regan. Come, my good lord, away   152 *out* on't   155 *taken* took

II, iii, 1 *heard* hear   10 *hairs in* hair with   19 *Sometimes* Sometime

II, iv, 3 *purpose in them* purpose   5 *Ha* How   7 *he* look, he   8 *heads* heels   25 *impose* purpose   34 *meiny* men   57 *here within* within   58 *here* there   59 *but* than   60 *None* no   61 *number* train   68 *twenty* a hundred   70 *following* following it   71 *upward* up the hill   74 *which serves and seeks* that serves   83 *stocks, fool* stocks   85 *have travelled all the night* travelled hard to-night   91 *Fiery? What quality* What fiery quality   97 *commands – tends – service* *commands her service   99 *Fiery? The fiery Duke* Fiery Duke   *that* that Lear   111 *Go tell* Tell   116 *O me, my heart, my rising heart! But down* O my heart, my heart   118 *knapped* rapped   132 *With* Of   135 *scant* slack   143 *his* *her   148 *you but* you   153 *Never* No   163 *blister* blast her pride   164 *mood is on* *mood –   186 *you yourselves* yourselves   189 *will you* wilt thou   217 *that's in* that lies within   227 *looked* look   230 *you* you are   251 *look* seem   258 *need* needs   267 *man* fellow   272 *And let* O let   293 *best* good   295 *high* *bleak   296 *ruffle* rustle   297 *scarce* not

III, i, s.d. *severally* at several doors   1 *Who's there besides* What's there beside   4 *elements* element   18 *note* art   20 *is* be   48 *that* *your   53–54 *King – in which your pain That way, I'll* this King – I'll this way, you that

III, ii, 5 *of* *to   7 *Strike* Smite   16 *tax* task   18 *Then* Now then   22 *will* have   *join* joined   42 *are* sit   49 *fear* force   50 *pudder* pother   54 *simular* simular man   55 *to* in   58 *concealing continents* concealed centers   64 *harder than the stones* hard than is the stone   71 *And* *That   73 *That's sorry* That sorrows   74 *has and* has   77 *Though* For   78 *boy* my good boy

III, iii, 4 *perpetual* their   12 *footed* landed   13 *look* seek   15 *If I* Though I   17 *strange things* some strange thing   23 *The* Then   *doth* do

III, iv, 4 *enter here* enter   6 *contentious* tempestuous   16 *home* sure   22 *enter here* enter   29 *storm* night   46 *blow the winds* *blows the cold wind   *Humh! go* Go   *bed* *cold bed   48 *Didst thou give all to thy* Hast given all to thy two   54 *porridge* pottage   57 *acold. O, do, de, do, de, do, de* acold   60 *there – and there again – and there* and there again   61 *Has his* What, his

62 *Wouldst* Didst   66 *light* fall   74 *Alow, alow, loo, loo* Alo, lo, lo   77 *words' justice* *words justly   94 *says suum, mun* hay   96 *Thou* Why, thou   *a* thy   98 *more than* *more but   100 *Ha! here's* here's   104 *contented ; 'tis* content; this is   108 *foul* foul fiend   110 *squints* *squemes (i.e. squinies?)   132 *Smulkin* Snulbug   148 *same* most   152 *him once more* him   162 *mercy, sir* mercy   173 *tower came* town come

III, v, 9 *letter which* *letter   11 *this* his

III, vi, 68 *Or bobtail* *Bobtail   69 *him* them   71 *leaped* *leap   72 *Do, de, de, de. Sessa* Loudla doodla   76 *these hard hearts* this hardness   78 *You will* You'll   *Persian* Persian attire   80 *here and rest* here   82 *So, so. We'll go to supper i' th' morning* So, so, so. We'll go to supper i' th' morning. So, so, so   93 *up, take up* up the King

III, vii, 3 *traitor* villain   23 *Though well* Though   32 *I'm none* I am true   42 *answered* answerer   53 *answer* first answer   58 *stick* *rash (meaning 'rip')   59 *bare* lowed   62 *rain* rage   63 *stern* *dearn (meaning 'drear')   65 *subscribe* *subscribed   73 *served you* served   79 *Nay* Why   81 *you have* *yet have you   86 *enkindle* unbridle   87 *treacherous villain* villain

IV, i, 4 *esperance* experience   9 *But who comes* Who's   10 *poorly led* parti, eyd (*sic*)   14 *These fourscore years* This fourscore –   17 *You* Alack, sir, you   36 *flies to* flies are to th'   45 *Which* Who   52 *daub* dance   54 *And yet I must. – Bless* Bless   57–58 *thee, good man's son* the good man

IV, ii, 17 *names* *arms   28 *My fool* A fool   *body* bed   29 *whistle* whistling   60 *seems* *shows   73 *thrilled* thralled

IV, iv, 10 *helps* can help   26 *importuned* important

IV, v, 15 *him, madam* him   40 *party* Lady

IV, vi, 1 *I* we   8 *In* With   46 *sir! Friend* sir   51 *Thou'dst* Thou hadst   65 *How is't* How   73 *make them* made their   78 *'twould* would it   89 *this piece of* this   91–92 *I' th' clout, i' th' clout* in the air, hah   96 *Goneril with a white beard* Goneril, ha Regan   104 *ague-proof* argue-proof   127 *sulphurous* sulphury   128 *consumption* consummation   130 *sweeten* *to sweeten   132 *Let me* Here   138 *thy* the   *see* see one   148 *this* the   150–51 *change places and, handy-dandy* Handy-dandy   159 *Thou* Thy blood   161 *clothes* rags   169 *Now, now, now, now* No, now   177 *wawl* wail   *Mark* Mark me   182 *felt. I'll put't in proof* felt   186 *dear daughter –* dear –   192 *a man a man* a man   195 *smug bridegroom* bridegroom   198 *Come* Nay   199 *running. Sa, sa,*

sa, sa running   207 *sound* sense   217 *tame to* lame by   224 *old*
most   237 *ballow* bat   246 *English* *British   252 *these* his
264 *servant* *servant, and for you her own for venture (*sic*)
277 *severed* *fencèd

IV, vii, 16 *jarring* hurrying   32 *opposed* exposed   *jarring* *war-
ring   36 *enemy's* injurious   58 *hand* hands   59 *You* No, sir,
you   *mock me* mock   61 *upward, not an hour more nor less* upward   70 *I am! I am* I am   79 *killed* cured   84 *Pray you* Pray

V, i, 21 *heard* hear   36 *Pray* Pray you   46 *And machination ceases.
Fortune* Fortune   52 *true* great

V, ii, 1 *tree* bush

V, iii, 8 *No, no, no, no* No, no   25 *starved* starve   43 *I* We   62
might should   68 *addition* advancement   78 *him* him then
81 *thine* good   90 *Gloucester. Let the trumpet sound* Gloucester
91 *person* head   93 *make* prove   96 *medicine* poison   99 *the* thy
105 *My* This   110–11 *within the lists* in the host   113 *by* at
120 *name, your* name and   124 *cope* *cope withal   129–30 *my
privilege, The privilege of mine honors* the privilege of my tongue
136 *Conspirant* Conspicuate   138 *below thy foot* beneath thy
feet   144 *tongue* being   146 *rule* right   147 *Back* Here   152
practice *mere practice   153 *war* *arms   155 *Shut* *Stop   156
stop *stopple   *it. – Hold, sir* it   157 *name* thing   172 *plague*
*scourge   174 *right; 'tis true* truth   186 *we* with   191 *Their*
The   197 *our* my   223 *help! O, help* help   225 *of – O, she's
dead* of   226 *Who dead? Speak, man* Who, man? Speak   228
poisonèd; she confesses poisoned; she hath confessed   232
judgment justice   233 *is this* 'tis   252 *Edgar* Albany   258
Howl, howl, howl Howl, howl, howl, howl   270 *you murderers*
your murderous   274 *woman* women   281 *brag* bragged   *and*
or   283 *This is a dull sight. Are* Are   289 *first* life   306 *no, no,
no* no, no   308 *Thou'lt* O, thou wilt   309 *Never, never, never,
never, never* Never, never, never   310 *sir* sir. O, o, o, o   316 *He*
O, he   324 *Edgar* Albany   326 *hath* *have